A little Christmas wish . . .

So was it Christmas or wasn't it? *Maybe—maybe yesterday was only a dream!* Jessica thought, growing excited. *That's it: I dreamed the whole thing. It was just a horrible, incredibly long, and utterly realistic nightmare!*

Jessica decided she would try a little test. When she saw the results, she'd know whether she was reliving history. "Mom, Dad? Do you think I could borrow a little money? I really need a new dress to wear to the *party* tonight." She looked around the table. Nobody jumped up and protested, "What party!" or, "It's Christmas; nothing will be open!" Jessica felt a prickle on the back of her neck.

Does this mean what I think it means? That my wish last night came true? That yesterday never really happened, and I'm getting a second chance?

Jessica grabbed a section of the newspaper. "December 24" was written at the top. It was true: It was Christmas Eve all over again!

Visit the Official Sweet Valley Web Site on the Internet at:

http://www.sweetvalley.com

SWEET VALLEY TWINS

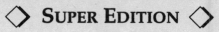

◇ SUPER EDITION ◇

The Year without Christmas

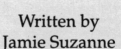

Written by
Jamie Suzanne

Created by
FRANCINE PASCAL

BANTAM BOOKS
NEW YORK • TORONTO • LONDON • SYDNEY • AUCKLAND

RL 4, 008-012

THE YEAR WITHOUT CHRISTMAS
A Bantam Book / December 1997

*Sweet Valley High® and Sweet Valley Twins® are
registered trademarks of Francine Pascal.*

Conceived by Francine Pascal.

*Produced by Daniel Weiss Associates, Inc.
33 West 17th Street
New York, NY 10011.*

Cover art by Bruce Emmett.

ISBN: 0-553-48348-X

Published simultaneously in the United States and Canada

*Bantam Books are published by Bantam Books, a division of Bantam
Doubleday Dell Publishing Group, Inc. Its trademark, consisting of the
words "Bantam Books" and the portrayal of a rooster, is Registered in the
U.S. Patent and Trademark Office and in other countries. Marca
Registrada. Bantam Books, 1540 Broadway, New York, New York 10036.*

PRINTED IN THE UNITED STATES OF AMERICA

OPM   0 9 8 7 6 5 4 3 2 1

To Cameron Robert Grant

One

◇

"Lila, you go first." Jessica Wakefield held the big hat full of tiny scraps of paper out to her best friend.

This was the first day of Sweet Valley Middle School's Christmas vacation. In two days, Jessica and her twin sister, Elizabeth, were hosting a Christmas Eve party. Everyone they had invited was now gathered around Jessica in the Wakefields' living room. They were drawing names out of a hat to see whom they would be "Secret Santa" for.

"Well, naturally. Don't I *always* go first?" Lila Fowler asked as she swept her long brown hair over her shoulder.

Jessica smiled sweetly. Even though Lila was her best friend, sometimes Lila's constant bragging drove Jessica crazy. She had to fight the urge, but Jessica decided not to say anything, because she wanted Mike McClusky to think she was a kind, generous person.

Mike had moved to Sweet Valley from Florida only about a month ago. Jessica didn't know him very well yet, but she could tell that he thought she was cute. That much was obvious from the way he kept smiling at her from his seat across the room next to Lila.

Jessica thought *he* was an absolute dreamboat. He had wavy blond hair and gorgeous bright green eyes. He was taller than most of the boys in the seventh grade, although he was in the sixth. He also seemed to have a great sense of humor. Right now, he was rolling his eyes, and Jessica had to stifle a giggle.

"Make sure you pick the *best* name out of the hat, Lila," Aaron Dallas joked from across the room. Aaron was Jessica's sort-of boyfriend, and he was funny and very cute. But Jessica didn't even bother to laugh at his joke. Ever since Mike had moved to town, she had eyes only for him.

Jessica's friends from the Unicorn Club—a group of the prettiest and most popular girls at Sweet Valley Middle School—were sitting on one side of the living room. Elizabeth's friends—mostly from the sixth-grade newspaper, *Sixers*, and other projects she was involved in—were sitting on the other. The two groups of friends didn't always get along, but they were getting along today. The holiday spirit had infected everyone.

Lila rummaged in the felt hat and pulled out a slip of paper. Her eyes widened as she read off the name to herself. Jessica wondered who she'd picked. *Me?* Jessica guessed hopefully. As Sweet Valley's resident millionaire, Lila would be the perfect person to have as a Secret Santa. She'd probably ignore the ten-dollar spending limit they'd set and go ahead and buy Jessica something really expensive and fabulous.

"Who did you get, Lila?" Ellen Riteman asked.

"It's a secret," Elizabeth Wakefield said with a smile. "That's why it's called *Secret* Santas."

"Oh." Ellen giggled, turning beet red. "Right."

Jessica walked around the circle of friends, holding the hat in front of each one and waiting for them to pick a name.

"Cool!" Aaron exclaimed as he read his slip of paper. "This is going to be easy."

"This isn't," Ken Mathews complained. "I'll be shopping for hours."

"Oh, man," Winston Egbert groaned as he made his selection. "Can I pick again?"

"No!" Jessica said. "Definitely not." Really, if the boys were going to be such whiners about the whole thing, then maybe they shouldn't be invited to her party. She hoped none of them had picked *her* name. But, of course, if they had, they wouldn't be groaning.

Anyway, if a guy was going to choose her name, then she wanted it to be Mike McClusky. It would be so romantic if he were her Secret Santa! He'd give her a much better present than any of those other guys, because he'd truly and deeply care whether she liked the gift or not.

Jessica held the hat toward her twin. "Go ahead, Elizabeth. Your turn." She smiled.

Elizabeth took a name out of the hat. When she read it, her eyes widened in surprise. She looked stunned, in fact. Then she recovered, looking up at the group with a broad smile. "Great! This is going to be a real challenge."

I wonder who she got, Jessica thought. *I'll have to ask her later.* Even though the Secret Santas were supposed to be top secret, Elizabeth couldn't keep that information to herself forever. After all, she and Jessica were identical twins, and that meant they should share everything.

Of course, just because they looked identical, with long blond hair and blue-green eyes, that didn't mean they did everything exactly the same way. For instance, Elizabeth probably wouldn't even want to tell Jessica who she'd picked. She'd act all honorable and refuse to break the rules. That is, until Jessica convinced her to spill the beans.

Jessica lived for breaking rules. She'd be the first to tell Elizabeth whom *she* was Secret Santa for. Jessica believed in sharing crucial information. What good were secrets—about Santa or anything else—if you couldn't share them with somebody?

"You go next," Elizabeth said, holding the hat toward Jessica.

"OK," Jessica said, excited. She rummaged around in the hat. *Please pick Mike's name, please pick Mike's name. . . .* She grasped a scrap of paper and opened it.

ELIZABETH WAKEFIELD was written in block letters.

Elizabeth! I can't tell her who I'm Secret Santa for now! thought Jessica. What was worse, how was Jessica going to keep the news a secret from her twin, when they were living in the same house? In rooms next door to each other? Sharing the same bathroom? "Can I—can I pick again?" she stammered.

"No," Winston said, looking smug. "Definitely not!"

Jessica frowned. "All right, but this really *isn't* fair."

"Come on, Jessica—you have to get into the spirit of the thing," Elizabeth said. "It doesn't matter who you pick. It's the thought that goes into the gift for them that's important. The challenge of trying to figure out what someone likes is what makes it fun. And in the end I'll bet we'll all be closer friends."

Jessica smiled weakly. That was such an Elizabeth thing to say. *She* wouldn't have to keep the biggest, most tantalizing secret in the world! Jessica shook the hat, rustling around the few remaining scraps. Well, just because she hadn't chosen Mike's name, that didn't mean he couldn't choose *hers*. *Anyway, it's much better to receive than to give, isn't it?* Jessica reminded herself.

She held the hat toward Mike. "Your turn!"

He rubbed his hands together. "Stand back, everybody. Santa Claus has come to town!"

"From Florida?" Amy Sutton laughed.

"Hey, it's sunnier than the North Pole," Mike said with a smile.

And the Santas in Florida are much cuter, Jessica thought.

Mike pulled a name out of the hat. He opened the slip of paper and read it to himself. "Interesting. Very interesting." He looked up from the piece of paper and smiled at Jessica, who was still standing in front of him, hat in hand. He stuffed the paper scrap into his back pocket.

"What's so interesting?" Jessica asked him.

"Oh, nothing." He shrugged. "I think I'm going to have fun with this one, though."

"Fun? Really?" Jessica asked eagerly.

"Sure! It's like Elizabeth said. We'll *all* be closer friends after we're Secret Santas," Mike said, grinning.

Closer friends with Mike McClusky? Jessica couldn't think of anything she'd like better for Christmas.

"So, what's your party going to be like?" Mandy Miller asked. She, Amy Sutton, Jessica, Elizabeth, and Lila had stayed at the Wakefield house to help clean up after everyone had left. Even though the group of friends had just gathered to have snacks and pick names out of a hat, they had still managed to make something of a mess of the living room.

"I was thinking that we could do something really modern for the party," Jessica replied.

"Modern?" Elizabeth asked, a stack of dirty paper cups in her hand. "What does that mean?"

"Jessica's going to arrive in a UFO," Lila joked. "Wearing a crinkly gold space suit."

"No, I'm not!" Jessica laughed. "I said *modern*, not *futuristic*."

"Christmas in Space . . . hey, that sounds like a movie title." Amy grinned.

"Intergalactic Christmas," Mandy added. "Part Four!"

"What I meant was modern as in . . . classy. Adult," Jessica explained. "Sophisticated. After

all, it's not like we're in elementary school anymore. We don't want vanilla cupcakes with
sprinkles on them; we want something nice!"

"I always loved those cupcakes," Mandy said.
"Actually, I just loved to lick the frosting off of
them."

Elizabeth giggled. "You know, I was kind of
hoping we could have an old-fashioned
Christmas party," she said. "Sitting by the fireplace, singing carols, stringing popcorn and
cranberries to decorate the tree—"

"No way!" Jessica protested. She'd never
heard anything more childish in her life. Did
Elizabeth think they were still in the first grade?
"Everyone does that!"

"So?" Elizabeth shrugged. "That's because it's
fun."

"No, it's because people aren't original
enough," Jessica said. "But believe me—I've got
plenty of one-of-a-kind ideas to make this a
once-in-a-lifetime party."

"You might have the ideas, but we don't have
that much time," Elizabeth said. "The great
thing about an old-fashioned Christmas is that
you don't have to buy a lot of stuff or make too
many arrangements."

"It might be tough to pull off some of my
ideas. But since when are you afraid of a little
hard work?" Jessica asked her twin. Elizabeth
was always making *her* look terrible, because of

the amount of work she did helping out with chores around the house. In fact, she was doing it right now, with the dirty cups and napkins. Was Elizabeth going to get lazy just in time for the party? "It'll be worth it—especially if a little work can make things seem nice." Jessica walked over to the couch and plumped up the pillows, just to make her point.

"I don't mind the work," Elizabeth replied. "I can't wait to have all of you guys here for the party," she added, turning to her friends. She went on, "But have you asked Mom and Dad about this yet, Jessica? I don't think they're expecting us to have a . . . formal party."

"Well, that's because we haven't talked about it yet. But once we do, I'm sure they'll love my ideas just as much as you do," Jessica said.

"I haven't heard your ideas yet," Elizabeth pointed out.

"Well, when you hear them, you'll love them," Jessica said.

Elizabeth looked at Amy, who was rolling her eyes. Elizabeth smiled. "OK, but you'll have to reveal your secret soon," Elizabeth said. "We only have three days."

Two days is plenty of time, because I've got everything planned, Jessica thought. *And our party's going to be amazing!*

Early the following morning, Elizabeth stared

in the window of Valley Fashions. She hadn't had a chance to start her Secret Santa shopping the day before, which was too bad because she was going to need a head start on this assignment.

Not that reindeer sweater—it's not cool enough. Not those black sparkling shoes—she already has at least three pairs. She probably doesn't own a mannequin . . . but why would she want to?

Elizabeth sighed and started walking to the next store in the mall. What in the world was she going to buy the girl who already had everything? She still couldn't believe she'd picked Lila Fowler's name out of the hat. Talk about Mission Impossible! She and Lila were not exactly friends, and Lila was the pickiest person on the planet. She probably didn't even own anything that was worth less than ten dollars, including her toothbrush.

Why couldn't I have picked someone easy, like Amy? Amy Sutton was Elizabeth's closest friend, aside from Jessica. Elizabeth would know just what to buy Amy. *Or I could have gotten Jessica's name . . . or even Winston's. . . . Anyone but Lila!*

Elizabeth reminded herself of what she'd told Jessica: It didn't matter what you bought, it was the spirit of giving that counted. She believed that with all her heart.

The question was, did Lila?

Lila would probably expect her Secret Santa to go way over the ten-dollar spending limit. Or else she'd expect the perfect ten-dollar gift, whatever *that* was. Elizabeth had no idea where to find it. She could make something, but if she did, Lila would probably laugh out loud and embarrass Elizabeth in front of everyone at her very own party. She could just picture Lila's reaction now: "Gee, thanks, Elizabeth. . . . What *is* it?"

Then she'd flip her hair over her shoulder, give Elizabeth a snobby look, and everyone would crack up.

Santa Claus probably faces challenges like this every year, Elizabeth consoled herself. *Especially when he flies over Lila Fowler's house!*

Two

Later that afternoon, the other Wakefield twin opened the doors to the south entrance of the Valley Mall and strode in. Jessica felt a little self-conscious. Going to the mall by herself was sort of creepy. She usually went with her friends in the Unicorn Club, or at least with Lila or Elizabeth. She felt kind of shy as she passed by crowds of Sweet Valley High students walking in groups. She wanted to tell them that it wasn't as if she didn't have anyone to shop with. She had tons of friends! She just couldn't hang out with them today, that was all. She needed to be alone. She couldn't let anyone find out who she was shopping for. Not even Elizabeth. Because it *was* Elizabeth.

Look on the bright side, Jessica told herself.

Picking a present for Elizabeth would be a cinch. *I could shop for Elizabeth with my brain tied behind my back*, she thought as she walked past all of her favorite stores.

Red and green signs were all over the mall: 20% Off Everything for Christmas!

Jessica grinned. Her strategy of waiting until the last possible minute to buy Elizabeth's Secret Santa gift had worked out perfectly. Well, it hadn't exactly been a strategy. She had tried to shop for Elizabeth the day before, but it hadn't quite worked out. Jessica had ended up with a bottle of silver nail polish, some new lip gloss, and a pair of patent leather shoes to wear to the party. She was sure that Mike McClusky would be very impressed with everything she had bought—it had been a very successful shopping trip. Just not in the way she had planned. But that was OK. In fact, it was great, since she didn't have to hide anything at home because she hadn't bought anything yet. And now she was going to save money by buying her gift late too!

The mall was packed with last-minute shoppers, looking frenzied and upset as they rushed from store to store. Really, Jessica didn't see why they were so stressed out. There were two whole shopping days left until Christmas. There was plenty of time to get everything done without knocking people down with giant bags of toys or scowling as they passed by. Had everyone forgotten the spirit of Christmas, or what?

Jessica dodged a man who was carrying a stack of boxes so high, he couldn't see over the top. Three women pushing baby carriages and looking very determined were right behind him, and Jessica leaped backward, out of the way, before they ran over her feet.

She found herself standing in the doorway of Sweet Valley Sports. *I wonder if there's anything Elizabeth would like in here,* she thought, wandering into the store. Jessica didn't feel like going back into the mall until it was safer. Maybe when everyone stopped for lunch in the food court, she could make a break for it. *This is probably why Santa Claus moved to the North Pole in the first place—to avoid the crowds,* Jessica decided.

Jessica strolled past the skis and surfboards and headed for the clothing department in the back of the store. When she saw who was shopping in the women's department, she nearly keeled over.

"Mike?" she asked softly. When he didn't respond, she tugged at his coat sleeve. "Mike?"

"Jessica!" He looked startled. "Uh, what are you doing here?"

"Looking for my Secret Santa present," Jessica said. "You too?" *Is that why you're in the girls' section, because you're picking out something for me?* she wondered hopefully.

"No, no . . . not for Secret Santa," Mike said. "Actually, I'm . . . well . . . looking for a present for my sister."

"You have a sister? How old is she?" Jessica asked.

"Uh . . . fifteen," Mike said. "No—fourteen."

He doesn't remember how old she is? Maybe that's because she doesn't exist! He's just making this up to hide the truth—that he's buying a gift for me.

"Really? That's the same age as my brother. He goes to Sweet Valley High," Jessica said. "Maybe he knows her?"

"Oh, I don't think so. We've only been in town a few weeks, you know," Mike said. "Besides, uh, she's really shy."

"Well, what's her name?" Jessica asked.

"Miranda. Miranda McClusky." Mike's face turned pink. "Of course we *would* have the same last name, wouldn't we?"

"Not necessarily," Jessica said, thinking of some of her friends whose parents were remarried. If Miranda existed, Jessica would just bet that she *wished* she had a different last name, though. Miranda McClusky? What a mouthful! "Anyway, what were you thinking of getting her?"

"Well, I can never remember what size she is, so I thought one of these adjustable caps would be a good idea," Mike said. "One of these with the names of the women's basketball teams on them."

"Personally, I love basketball," Jessica said, trying to give him a hint. "Sometimes my friends and I like to get together and play. We even started a team last season—the Honeybees."

"Really?" Mike seemed interested. "Like, uh, who was on it? Anyone I know?"

"Sure! Elizabeth, and Mandy, and Ellen," Jessica said. "And me, of course. I have a great jump shot." *Well, that one I made during our big game really helped anyway.*

"You . . . and your friends, like, um, Ellen and whoever. You guys know about those new pro women's teams, right?" Mike asked.

"Oh, sure," Jessica said. "Aren't those teams awesome?"

"Yeah. So what do you think of this hat?" Mike held up a purple cap with the Utah Unicorns' logo on the front of it.

Jessica grinned. "I love it!" How did he know to pick such a perfect gift for her? She had practically founded the Unicorn Club single-handedly.

OK, so maybe she had just joined it, not founded it, but Jessica was one of the most important members in the club. How did Mike know that already? He'd only transferred to Sweet Valley a few weeks ago. Of course, he had probably noticed that purple was one of her favorite colors—she and the other Unicorn Club members tried to wear something purple every day.

"Really? You think it's a good present for my sister?" Mike asked.

"Definitely," Jessica told him. "I'm sure your . . . *sister* would love it as much as I do."

Mike looked a bit nervous. He started picking up other hats and looking at them.

Jessica figured she was making him uncomfortable, hovering over him while he tried to pick out her Secret Santa gift. She'd have to change the subject. "So, the party's going to be a lot of fun," she told him. "We're going to have music and tons of great food. And then we're going to clear out all the presents and stuff and have dancing."

"Sounds like fun." Mike smiled. "I should be there at seven o'clock, right?"

"Right." Jessica looked around the store. "Well, I should probably take off. I still have to buy my Secret Santa present."

"OK," Mike said. "See you tomorrow night."

I can't wait! Jessica thought. *This is going to be the best party ever.* She could see it now: She and Mike, sitting in front of the Christmas tree . . . she would pretend to be surprised when she opened his gift, he would pretend he wasn't already crazy about her. . . .

"Jessica?" Mike waved a baseball cap in front

of her face. "I said, I'll see you tomorrow night?"

"Oh, um, yeah. Great! Don't be late!" Jessica walked out of the store. She'd never been looking forward to a party more in all her life!

Jessica's little conversation with Mike had made her so happy, she was practically skipping through the mall. She paused outside Total Trends as a giant earring tree in the middle of the store caught her eye. Earrings! Why hadn't she thought of it before?

Ever since she and Elizabeth had had their ears pierced not too long ago, they'd loved giving each other earrings as gifts. And Jessica would be able to find something for ten dollars too. Maybe even under ten dollars. With the leftover money, she could buy Elizabeth a matching bracelet. Or maybe even get her another pair of earrings from the 2-for-$10 rack.

She walked in and started scanning the spinning racks of earrings. There were so many pairs, it was a bit overwhelming. Gold hoops, silver hoops, dangling stones, rhinestone studs . . . Finally, she spotted a pair of silver earrings shaped like miniature typewriters. Perfect! Elizabeth loved to write. Jessica took them off the rack and held them against her ear. They were very cute—definitely Elizabeth's kind of thing. Jessica turned them over. $8.99. *Bingo!*

She marched up to the counter and was about to ask the clerk for a gift box when a special

Hoop It Up for the Holidays! display caught her eye.

"Wow!" she cried, picking up a pair of delicate silver ball-shaped earrings. "They look just like tiny ornaments!"

"Aren't they cute?" the clerk asked. "Did you see these, with the glitter?" She reached around the other side of the display and pulled off a pair of earrings.

Jessica's eyes widened. "These would go *perfectly* with my new nail polish. It's silver glitter too."

"Then you'll have to get them," the clerk said with a smile. "Do you have a special party to go to?"

"A very special party. I'm hosting it, actually," Jessica said, admiring the earrings as she held one up against her ear. "How much are these?"

"Ten dollars," the clerk said. "I'm not trying to pressure you, but we only have a couple pairs left."

"Hmmm." Jessica looked in her wallet. She had only twelve dollars with her. If she bought the typewriter earrings for Elizabeth, she wouldn't have enough for the pair she wanted. And vice versa. She could buy the glittery earrings now and come back for the typewriter ones . . . or give Elizabeth a gift certificate with a picture of the typewriter earrings on it. . . .

Don't be ridiculous! Jessica told herself. *You can't do that. You'll get the earrings for Elizabeth now, then come back for the other ones.* But if there weren't any of the silver ornament earrings left, she'd be devastated. She had to have those earrings to match her nail polish.

"Do you really only have a few pairs of these left?" Jessica asked.

The clerk nodded. "Sorry."

"It's OK." Jessica stared at the two pairs of earrings. Maybe those little typewriters were a little *too* cute. Did she want a sister walking around with typewriters on her ears? Probably not. She might look like a study geek. And Jessica would be responsible for ruining Elizabeth's image—and her own image, by association.

"I'll take these," Jessica said, placing the ornament-shaped silver earrings on the counter.

"Do you need a box?" the clerk asked.

"No, these are for me. I'll . . . have to think about the other ones," Jessica said.

"Shall I hold them back here for you?"

"No, thanks," Jessica said. "That won't be necessary." *I'll find something much, much cooler for Elizabeth—tomorrow. When I come back to the mall to buy a new dress to complete my perfect outfit.*

Three

"Do you want to come in with me, Elizabeth?" Mrs. Wakefield asked, stepping out of the mini-van that afternoon. "It shouldn't take too long to copy this letter, but you never know. There might be a line."

"Sure, I'll come in," Elizabeth said, climbing out of her seat. Even though she still needed to find a present for Lila, Elizabeth was taking some time out to help her mother do some last-minute holiday errands such as grocery shopping for the party and, now, getting the family holiday newsletter photocopied.

"I think I'll have them make copies on both red and green paper this year," Mrs. Wakefield said. "Red for page one, green for page two."

"That sounds nice," Elizabeth said, holding

the door open for her mother. "Or you could save paper and have them put page two on the back of page one."

"That's a great idea," her mother said. "I didn't think of that. I'll be saving a few trees, with the quantity of newsletters we're planning to send."

"Or at least a few branches," Elizabeth joked as her mother stepped up to the counter to place her order.

"Oh, I don't know. Our list has so many people on it now, I might save an entire forest," Mrs. Wakefield said. "Good afternoon," she greeted the clerk. "Can you help me?"

While her mother took care of the photocopying, Elizabeth wandered around the shop. She loved looking at all the different kinds of paper and pens the store sold. There were at least twenty different bright-colored highlighting markers. Elizabeth took a few out of the giant plastic bin and experimented writing with them. Then she walked back over to the counter, where her mother was waiting.

A giant easel was placed on the counter. "The Perfect Christmas Gift!" it said in large letters. "A Personalized Calendar for Your Loved Ones. Just give us your photos, and we'll make a year-long calendar they'll never forget to check."

Elizabeth flipped through the display calendar, looking at the pictures for each month.

What a great idea, she thought, looking at all the personal reminders that had been inserted for special days, like birthdays and anniversaries. It would make a great gift for someone who was hard to shop for.

Someone . . . like Lila! she thought excitedly. *I could have a calendar made for Lila! I could use all the pictures I've collected so far this year for* Sixers. *And Jessica probably has a ton of other pictures of Lila, and of her and Lila together.*

But she didn't have time to get the calendar made—the display said to allow at least a week. *Then I'll just have to make it myself,* Elizabeth decided.

In fact, I won't make a calendar. I'll make her her very own personalized school yearbook—of all her closest friends! She'd buy a photo album, fill it with pictures, and write special, funny captions under each picture. . . . It was the perfect ten-dollar gift for somebody who already had everything she could ever want.

Elizabeth was sure that Lila would love her gift. She only hoped she'd have enough time to get it all done by tomorrow night! "Excuse me, do you sell photo albums?" she asked the manager behind the counter.

"We certainly do," she said. "They're right over there, next to the shipping supplies."

"Thanks," Elizabeth said.

"What do you need a photo album for?" Mrs.

Wakefield asked with a curious expression.

"For a present," Elizabeth said. "It's a secret, so I can't say."

"Aha! Secret Santa time." Her mother nodded. "Don't worry, I didn't see a thing."

"Come on, Jessica! Come on, Elizabeth! Time to make the final party plans!" Mr. Wakefield's voice boomed up the stairwell.

Jessica turned off her radio, grabbed her notebook, and rushed out of her room. She couldn't wait to share all her inspired ideas for the party with her mother and father. They were going to be so proud. She'd never planned anything in so much detail in her entire life.

"Elizabeth!" She pounded on her sister's door. "Come on!" She tried to turn the doorknob, but it was locked. What was Elizabeth doing with her door locked? Jessica wondered as she rattled the doorknob. *Probably wrapping more presents for me,* she thought with a smile.

"Hold on!" Elizabeth called. She slipped out of her room a few seconds later.

"What were you doing in there?" Jessica asked.

"Working on my Secret Santa present," Elizabeth said. "I can't talk about it, though. Amy already barged in on me and found out who it is, so I definitely can't tell you too."

"Oh." Jessica's heart sank. Then it wasn't

another gift for her. *Unless Elizabeth drew my name, just like I'd drawn hers . . . that would be kind of cool!* she thought excitedly. *Except that's impossible, because Mike picked my name. Didn't he?*

"How was your shopping trip at the mall?" Elizabeth asked. "Were you successful?"

"Very," Jessica said, hopping down the stairs. Well, successful for *her* anyway. "But I'll probably have to go back tomorrow for some last-minute stuff." She nearly crashed into Steven, who was standing at the bottom of the stairs, about to head up. "Watch it!" Jessica cried.

"*You* watch it," Steven said.

"No yelling. And where do you think you're going, Steven? I asked you to come to this meeting," Mr. Wakefield said.

"Why do I need to be there?" Steven asked.

"Because we need you to help with your sisters' party tomorrow night," Mr. Wakefield said.

"You mean . . . setting up chairs and vacuuming and stuff, right?" Jessica asked. "Steven's not actually going to *be* at the party."

"Not if I can help it," Steven said under his breath.

"Actually, Steven *will* be at the party," Mr. Wakefield said as the three kids followed their father into the living room, where their mother was sitting on the couch. "That is, if we can strike a deal. Steven, we'd like it if you'd work as a waiter at the party—"

"What? A waiter? But, Dad, he'll insult all my friends!" Jessica cried, horrified. "He can't be a waiter."

"That's fine with me—as if I want to wait on your friends!" Steven shook his head. "Forget it. No way."

"Come on, Steven, you haven't even heard what we want you to do. And if you work tomorrow night—which includes *not* insulting Jessica's and Elizabeth's friends—we'll pay you for it," Mr. Wakefield said.

"Money?" Steven's eyes lit up. "How much money?"

Mrs. Wakefield spoke up. "We'll pay you ten dollars an hour—with a bonus on top of that, if everything goes well. How does that sound?" she asked.

"Ten dollars an hour!" Jessica shrieked. "Mom, all he has to do is pour ginger ale into cups!"

"He'll be a big help to *us*," Mr. Wakefield said. "And the party should only last two to three hours, tops."

Jessica shook her head. "I don't think so. I'm planning on having it go very late."

"You are?" Elizabeth asked.

"Cool." Steven rubbed his hands together. "The later it goes, the more I rake in. Now, about my bonus, for everything going well?"

"Mom, do you seriously think everything

will go *well*, with Steven doing the work?"
Jessica asked. She swept her hair off her shoulder. "We might as well not *have* a waiter, if he's
the one we've got."

"Jessica, think of it this way: With Steven
helping, we'll be able to relax and enjoy the
party with our friends," Elizabeth pointed out.

"Yeah, Jessica, be quiet. You're just trying to
scam me out of my money," Steven said.

"I am not! I just don't want you to embarrass
me," Jessica said.

"I don't need to embarrass you," Steven said.
"You do a good enough job of that yourself."

Jessica glared at him. She didn't want him
anywhere near her Christmas party! But she decided to do the grown-up thing and ignore him.
She picked up her notebook. "All right, all right.
Let's move on. I don't want to waste any more
time talking about Steven."

"Hey!" Steven cried. "I'm the best topic of
conversation in this room!" He glanced at his
parents. "The best topic under thirty, that is."

"Because the way I see it, we have so much to
arrange, we need to get started right away,"
Jessica went on, ignoring him. "I've gone ahead
and made a list of all the things I want for the
party. Starting with the decorations. I saw this
TV show all about holiday parties."

"Uh-oh," Mr. Wakefield groaned.

"Dad! It's not what you're thinking. These

ideas are *good*," Jessica insisted. "First, we get a bunch of streamers and shiny silver and gold and red ribbons and . . ." She consulted her notes. "Fresh fallen fir boughs. And we lay them all around, on the stairs, on the dining room table—"

"Jessica, I don't think we can get fir boughs at this point," Mrs. Wakefield said. "The tree will be delivered tomorrow, and that's pretty much it."

"Oh. Well, I guess that's OK," Jessica said. "But that means we have to work even harder on our *other* decorations—like the ones for the table. Like the gold-painted placemats, and the green cloth napkins that we're going to fan into Christmas trees, and the reindeer we can make out of everyday wire hangers."

Steven burst out laughing. "Yeah, right."

"Jessica, that sounds like a lot of work. We don't need everything to be that fancy," Elizabeth said.

"Yes, we do. This party is a big deal! Besides, it's really easy," Jessica said. "I wrote down the directions."

"Jessica, that sounds nice, but we don't have time for all that. Anyway, that's for a more formal party," Mr. Wakefield observed.

"Can't we make this party formal?" Jessica asked. "It is Christmas Eve, after all."

"Yeah, and it *is* a group of sixth-graders, after

all," Steven said in a snobby tone. "When the clown shows up, make sure he's wearing a tuxedo, will you, Mother Dear?"

Elizabeth cracked up.

Jessica glared at her. Whose side was Elizabeth on anyway?

"OK, let's get back to the real world now and start some serious planning," Mrs. Wakefield began.

"I *was* planning it," Jessica argued. She tried to control the whining tone in her voice. "What's so bad about my ideas? You haven't even heard all of them yet."

Her mother shifted on the couch. "We haven't?"

"No. I was also thinking we could put some of those candles that float in water at everyone's place," Jessica said. "Alternating red and green. Then we'll put little gift bags on everyone's chair, like party favors, only they're full of really delicious, expensive chocolates and wrapped in gold and silver and green foil."

"I was thinking more like one large bowl of chocolate candy," Mr. Wakefield said, "and one giant red candle in the middle of the table."

"But, Dad, that's tacky!" Jessica protested.

"Jessica, it's a Christmas get-together, not the event of the century," Mrs. Wakefield said. "Now, come on. Let's be realistic."

"But I *am* being realistic," Jessica argued. *I'm not about to have a lame party at my very own house!* She'd never hear the end of it from Lila and Janet. And she'd never impress Mike either, if everyone sat around staring at a boring candle, munching on stale candy.

"Fine," she snapped. "Can we at least have some cool music, so we can dance? I was thinking Steven could be the DJ, we could clear out all this furniture, and maybe have a dance contest. We could give out special party favors that have to do with dancing and maybe a big gold trophy shaped like a pair of shoes. We could call our party . . . the Festive Dance of Noel."

"Um—" Mr. Wakefield started.

Steven interrupted. "And maybe you can dress up as one of Santa's elves and hand out bars of solid gold to all of your guests. That's another very simple and inexpensive idea."

Jessica narrowed her eyes at her brother. "I am not going to dress like an elf. I'm planning on wearing an evening gown," she said.

"An evening gown? Dancing?" Elizabeth shook her head. "I don't know, Jessica. . . ."

"What don't you know?" Jessica asked. "Everyone likes the chance to dress up once in a while."

"Sure, but not on one day's notice," Elizabeth said. "We didn't tell people they should dress up. Anyway, wouldn't you rather sing Christmas carols than dance?"

"No," Jessica said. "Elizabeth, I thought we

talked about this. I *thought* we agreed."

"No, we didn't agree," Elizabeth said.

"Then agree *now*," Jessica urged through gritted teeth.

"Jessica wants a modern Christmas party," Elizabeth explained, as if it were a truly bizarre concept. "But I think we should do something more old-fashioned."

"Yes, I like Elizabeth's idea," Mr. Wakefield said. "We were talking about it earlier. In fact, I've already gone ahead and made some arrangements in that direction."

"You have?" Jessica asked. "Without consulting *me?* Wait a second. This is *our* party—not just Elizabeth's." She turned to her twin. "I can't believe you spoke to Mom and Dad without me when you knew I had ideas for the party!"

"Jessica," Elizabeth began, "I just mentioned a few things that Mom and Dad already had in mind anyway. It's not like I went behind your back—"

"Yes, it is. It's exactly like that," Jessica replied. She snapped her notebook shut. "So what are the big plans everyone already knows about except me anyway?"

"Oh, it's nothing drastic, Jessica—don't worry," Mr. Wakefield said. But I've spoken to Winston Egbert, and he's agreed to accompany me on the accordion—"

"Ac-Accordion?" Jessica interrupted with a sputter. Was she hearing right? "Ac-Accompany you?" That wasn't drastic—that was disastrous!

"Yes. We thought we could lead everyone in some carols," Mr. Wakefield said. "I'll play my harmonica, and Winston will play the accordion."

"Dad, this isn't a *square* dance! This is a Christmas party!" Jessica yelled.

"Square dancing . . . hey, that really sounds like fun," Elizabeth said. "I didn't think of that, but—"

"Well, don't think of it anymore!" Jessica screeched. She stared at her sister with eyes practically popping out of her head. "Elizabeth, how could you even suggest something so dumb?"

"Jessica," Mrs. Wakefield said in a warning tone.

"Sorry," Jessica muttered. But what else was she supposed to say, when Elizabeth wanted to turn their elegant holiday party into a country hoedown?

"Jessica, relax. I was just kidding about the square dancing. But seriously, everyone likes to sing carols on Christmas Eve," Elizabeth said. "We'll have fun."

Jessica glared at Elizabeth. "You'll have fun, because you're getting your way. But I won't!"

"Come on, Jessica—it'll be great. We'll sing the carols, then we'll serve dinner. And we'll all trim the tree together." Elizabeth thought for a moment, then added, "Besides the ornaments we already have, we can get some cranberries and popcorn, and make chains of colored construction paper—"

"We've got a few bags of cranberries in the freezer. I bought too many at Thanksgiving," Mrs. Wakefield said. "And we already have some popcorn too. Now, the construction paper—"

"Are you *kidding?*" Jessica was aware that she was starting to sound obnoxious, but she didn't care. Mike McClusky was coming to her house. He was going to think she was a total nerd! She had to rescue this party! "This isn't day care! This is a sixth-grade Christmas party," she argued.

"Jessica, I don't think age matters when you're talking about Christmas parties. These ideas are timeless," Mrs. Wakefield said. "It sounds like a lot of fun to me. In fact, it sounds perfect," she said with a smile.

"Sure, it's perfect. Perfectly dorky," Jessica muttered.

"What was that, Jessica?" Mr. Wakefield asked. "You look upset."

"That's because I am! Why can't we ever do anything the way I want?" Jessica complained. "Who ever heard of polka music at a Christmas party? This is going to be terrible—I'll be humiliated! No one will ever come to one of my parties again!"

"Jessica, what is the matter with you? You've done nothing but complain all evening," Mrs. Wakefield said. "And I do not like your tone of voice. You ought to be grateful that we're letting you host this party, and you should be glad that you have so many friends who want to come. But if you think the party is going to be terrible, then maybe you should stay in your room instead of hosting it!"

Oops. The party won't be any fun if I'm stuck in my room, grounded. "I am grateful, Mom," Jessica insisted in her most sincere tone of voice, hoping she sounded convincing. "I am. And I'm sorry if I sounded disappointed. It's just that I had these ideas. . . ." She gazed wistfully at her notebook and let out a loud sigh. "This is supposed to be our party. Mine and Elizabeth's!"

"It still is," Elizabeth said.

"No, it isn't," Jessica turned to her twin. "It's *your* party. Everything is the way *you* want it. You haven't even considered *one* of my ideas," she complained. "Don't I count?"

"Of course you do, honey," Mrs. Wakefield said, and Elizabeth nodded. "All right, let's think a minute. How can we work an idea from your list into the old-fashioned Christmas plans. . . ." She tapped her finger against her chin.

"We could do the, um, reindeer shapes," Elizabeth said. "With pipe cleaners or whatever."

"I don't know if that's practical," Mrs. Wakefield said. "We could shape the napkins into trees . . . if we could figure out how."

"That stuff's too hard," Steven said. "You should go with the party favor idea. You know, bags of candy and stuff on people's chairs. I know I always like to get presents when I go to someone's house."

Jessica turned to her brother with a smile. "See? I told you it was a good idea. We'll buy gourmet chocolates and—"

"Jessica, gourmet chocolates can be pretty expensive," Mr. Wakefield said. "Just stick to the basics. You can get some simple candy and wrap it nicely, OK?"

"OK," Jessica sighed. It wouldn't be what she wanted, but it would be something.

"Tell you what, Jessica. I'll help," Steven offered.

"You will?" Jessica couldn't believe it.

"Sure." He leaned closer. "I don't want you guys to have the dweeb party of the year either. It might make *me* look bad, if stuff gets back to people at Sweet Valley High."

Finally! Jessica thought. *Someone on my side.* Maybe now the party wouldn't go down as the dorkiest in history. But if it did, that would be Elizabeth's fault!

"Thanks for your help, Steven. At least I can count on you." Jessica glared across the room at her twin. *Some* people couldn't be counted on at all!

Four

Jessica stretched her arms over her head and rolled over in bed, staring up at the ceiling. A car outside on the street honked its horn and Jessica frowned. Did they have to wake her up so early on Christmas Eve? It was a holiday, after all.

Wait a second. Christmas Eve? It's the day of the party! I still need to buy a dress for me and a present for Elizabeth! I'm in a rush.

Jessica tossed off the covers and climbed out of bed. From the bathroom in between her and Elizabeth's rooms, she heard the shower knobs squeak, the way they did whenever somebody turned them off. *Elizabeth's up and she already took a shower. I've got to get moving!*

As Jessica quickly changed from her flannel

pajamas into a pair of jeans and a sweater, she heard her parents walk by in the hallway, on their way downstairs.

"Well, I don't know if we should give the kids his cards this morning or tomorrow morning," her mother was saying.

"Bob wants them to open the cards on Christmas Eve. There's really no point in waiting until tomorrow," her father replied.

What are they talking about? Jessica wondered as she slid her feet into a pair of brown suede clogs. It sounded like they'd gotten their annual Christmas cards from Uncle Bob. So what was the big decision?

She opened her door and walked downstairs to the kitchen. Steven and Elizabeth were already seated at the breakfast table. "Good morning, everyone," she said cheerfully, trying to forget that the last time she'd seen her parents, they'd been implying she was acting rude. As if wanting all of her friends to have a great time at the party was acting rude!

"Good morning, Jessica," Mrs. Wakefield greeted her.

"Hi there." Mr. Wakefield slid into a seat opposite Steven and opened the morning newspaper to the business section.

Steven looked at her over the top of the sports section. "What happened to you?"

"What do you mean?" Jessica asked.

"I think you should go back to bed," Steven said. "You could use a few more hours' worth of beauty sleep."

"And you could use a few more years' worth," Jessica replied, rubbing her eyes. "But I don't have time to go into all that right now. I need to ask you a question."

"I know, I know. Can you borrow money from me for your last-minute shopping? The answer is no," Steven said.

"That's not the question." Jessica took a sip of orange juice. Of course, she did need to find some more money, but she was planning to ask her parents about that. "Do you know someone at school named Miranda McClusky?"

Steven shook his head. "No."

"You don't know her? But does she go to Sweet Valley High?" Jessica asked.

"How should I know? And why do you care?" Steven asked.

"Because her brother is in our class. And he was talking about her, and she'd be in the freshman class with you," Jessica said.

"So?" Steven muttered.

"Never mind. I was just trying to make conversation, but if you're going to be such a grump, forget about it."

"Fine," Steven said, "I will."

"Just make sure you cheer up by tonight. And don't spill anything on anyone," Jessica said. "My friends are going to be wearing really nice clothes."

Steven looked across the table at Jessica with menacing eyes, as if he were about to jump over and strangle her. "Don't worry about me," he said in a bitter tone. "I'll be fine. I won't embarrass you."

"Yeah, right," Jessica mumbled. "You're still helping with the party favors, aren't you?" she reminded him.

"I was going to, but now I'm not so sure," Steven muttered.

"Please?" Jessica asked. "I have so much to do today. I couldn't possibly get all the candy and the bags and—"

"OK, I'll do it," Steven said with a loud sigh. "Just this once. But you'll owe me—big-time!"

"You still owe me from two years ago, when I helped you with your Halloween costume," Jessica said.

"Oh, please," Steven said.

"Well, you do," Jessica said.

"You kids go ahead and get all your arguments out of the way now," Mr. Wakefield said. "Then we won't have any problems tonight."

"The last thing you want to do is argue in front of your guests," Mrs. Wakefield added helpfully.

"Don't worry, Mom. When everyone shows up, I'll be cool, I promise," Steven said. "But next time I have a party, I want Jessica and Elizabeth to help out."

"No problem," Elizabeth told him, smiling.

"Fine, as long as I get paid the same amount you are," Jessica said. "Unless, unlike you, I actually *have* a busy social life and I'm not free that night. But getting back to the money issue . . . Mom, Dad? Do you think I could borrow a little? I really need a new dress to wear to the party tonight."

"Aha!" Steven cried. "I knew that question would come up eventually."

"You're buying a new dress?" Elizabeth asked.

"Of course," Jessica said. "Why not?"

Elizabeth shrugged. "No reason. But personally, I think I have too many clothes. Last night, I was building up a huge collection of clothes I never wear or that don't fit anymore, to give away to charity. Do you have some to add?"

"No," Jessica said. What was her twin thinking? "Are you crazy? I need all of them." That didn't sound very nice, but Jessica didn't care. She was still angry with Elizabeth.

"Well, Sweet Valley Home Services is having a special clothing drive, because of the holidays," Elizabeth said. "So if you come across anything . . ."

"I won't," Jessica said. She knew Elizabeth wanted her to help, but she wasn't about to do anything to make Elizabeth happy. Elizabeth had already tried to ruin the party by insisting on having everything her way. Now she wanted Jessica to wear an old, outdated outfit too? Forget it!

Jessica turned back to her parents. "So what do you say, Mom and Dad? Can you advance me a little on my January allowance?"

"No," Mr. Wakefield said abruptly.

"Not a chance," Mrs. Wakefield added.

Jessica was too stunned to speak for a minute. Not even a *chance?* First she had to deal with her sister's criticism, and now the Scrooge bug had bitten her parents? Wasn't Christmas the season for giving?

"However, your uncle Bob might be able to help you out." Mr. Wakefield slid an envelope across the table to Jessica, and then gave one each to Elizabeth and Steven.

Jessica ripped open the envelope. "Season's Greetings to My Niece," the card said. *Blah, blah, blah . . .* Jessica skimmed the corny poem on the front, then opened the card. A check for fifty dollars fell onto the table. Jessica could hardly believe her eyes. "But Uncle Bob usually only gives us ten dollars!" Jessica said.

"You're complaining?" Steven scoffed. "I'm not."

"Neither am I!" Elizabeth said. "Wow, how generous. I think I'll add this to my donation to the clothing drive."

"I'll be happy to drive you and your stuff over there later today," Mrs. Wakefield said. "But first, I think we ought to bake some more cookies for the party tonight. I'm afraid we don't have nearly enough."

"Oh, OK," Elizabeth said. "That'll be fun. You're going to help, right, Jessica?"

"No, I can't. I have to go to the mall," Jessica said. "I have more shopping to do. You know— presents. For my Secret Santa person."

"And for yourself," Steven mumbled.

"Maybe you could go to the mall this afternoon instead, Jessica," Mrs. Wakefield said. "We could really use your help in the kitchen."

"But the stores are going to close early, because it's Christmas Eve," Jessica said.

"Then I guess you'll just have to wear some old outfit. Like one of the ones you bought way back . . . last month?" Elizabeth said.

Jessica wrinkled her nose. "Maybe you want to wear an old-fashioned dress to our old-fashioned party, but I don't. Anyway, couldn't you just *buy* some more cookies with your fifty dollars instead of giving it away?"

Elizabeth folded her arms across her chest. "For that matter, couldn't you?"

"Well . . . no, because I need a new dress," Jessica said. If Elizabeth wasn't going to budge, then neither was she.

"If you're not going to help us this morning,

then please make sure you're home this afternoon to help, all right? Elizabeth can't do all the work herself," Mr. Wakefield said. "Jessica, you can at least get everything together to make the cranberry and popcorn strands for the tree."

"Oh, sure, Dad. No problem. I'll be home just as soon as I find the perfect dress," Jessica promised. She lifted the check to her lips and kissed it. *Thank you, Uncle Bob! At least someone in the Wakefield family understands my needs.*

Jessica turned back and forth in front of the mirror later that morning.

"It looks adorable on you," Danielle, the store clerk at Valley Fashions, told her. "I love that belt."

Jessica adjusted the shiny black patent leather belt. It contrasted nicely with the red dress. "It'll go perfectly with my black patent leather shoes," she said.

"Oh, definitely," Danielle agreed. "And it really fits you well. The red looks great with your blond hair. And everyone knows, red is *the* color to wear to holiday parties this year."

"It is?" Jessica asked eagerly. "I mean, yeah, I'd heard that too. Well, uh, how do you think this dress will look with silver? I have some silver accessories already picked out."

"Silver and red are wonderful together," Danielle said. "Add your black shoes, and maybe a black ribbon in your hair . . . you'll be the belle of the ball."

Jessica stared at Danielle's reflection in the mirror. "The what?"

"Oh, sorry. I meant, the prettiest girl in the room," Danielle said. "That was an old-fashioned expression."

"That's OK," Jessica said. "My sister's trying to make this an old-fashioned party."

"In that outfit? You'll look anything but," Danielle assured her.

"Then I'll take it," Jessica declared, smiling triumphantly. "You said thirty percent off, right?"

Danielle nodded. "Yes, it's our special last-minute sale. You've got perfect timing."

"I always thought so," Jessica said proudly. Wait until Mike saw her in that dress. He'd forget all about the silly carol singing and homemade cookies. All he'd be able to see was *her.* She was going to be the belle of the ball. Whatever that meant.

"Jessica! Hi!" Mandy Miller said.

"Hey, Mandy," Jessica said, stopping as she was halfway out the door of the mall.

"Wow, I thought you'd be home all day getting ready for the party," Mandy commented.

"I'm going there now," Jessica said, looking at Ellen Riteman and Janet Howell, who were with Mandy. "I hope you guys are going to have a great time. It's not going to be exactly how I wanted it, but you know how it is. Parents." She wrinkled her nose to show her displeasure. "Actually, more like sisters. Elizabeth's being such a pain, you wouldn't believe it."

Janet rolled her eyes. "Don't worry, Jessica, we'll make the best of it. As long as all the Unicorns are there, it's automatically a good time." Even though Janet was an eighth-grader, Jessica had invited her to the party because she was one of her best friends—and the president of the Unicorn Club. She was also Lila's cousin.

"So, what did you buy?" Janet asked. "Your Secret Santa gift?"

"No," Jessica said, suddenly realizing she had left the mall without picking up something for Elizabeth again. At the moment, she didn't exactly care. She was still furious with Elizabeth for mocking her ideas. She'd show Elizabeth who had good ideas when she showed up in the hottest dress of anyone at the party. "Check this out." Jessica took the red dress out of the bag and held it up against her body.

"Wow, that's . . . cute!" Ellen said.

"Definitely a holiday party dress," Mandy said, nodding appreciatively.

Jessica looked at Janet, waiting for her to say something nice too. But Janet was staring at the dress with a strange expression on her face. "Is that what you're wearing?" she asked. "Really?"

"Sure," Jessica said. "Why? Don't you like it?"

"Well, kind of . . . but maybe that's because I like Santa Claus," Janet said slowly.

"Huh?" Jessica asked.

"Are you going to wear black patent leather boots to match? And a big white beard too?" Janet asked.

"You know, I didn't see it at first, but now that you mention it . . . ," Ellen began.

Jessica turned the dress back and forth, examining it. "What are you guys talking about?" Did it have a mini-Santa appliqué that she hadn't noticed?

"No, wait—I get it!" Janet cried, fingering the dress material. "This isn't a man's outfit."

"Of course not," Jessica said. "It's a dress."

"Yeah. It's the dress that *Mrs.* Claus wears every Christmas Eve!" Janet said.

Ellen giggled. "You're right, Janet. It *does* sort of look like Mrs. Claus."

"Don't listen to them," Mandy told Jessica. "It doesn't look like Mrs. Claus at all." She stepped back, gazing at the dress.

"Come on, Mandy—don't you see it? It definitely looks like something that at least *Miss* Claus would wear. Claus-o-rama!" Janet giggled.

"Well, maybe a little." Mandy wrinkled her nose, giving Jessica a sympathetic look.

Janet laughed. "Oh well, Jessica. It's a Christmas party, so I guess you might as well dress the part."

Jessica hurriedly stuffed the dress back into the bag. She hadn't *had* to invite Janet. She'd done it out of the kindness of her heart. That, plus the fact that Janet would never have forgiven her if she hadn't. And this was the thanks she got? Mocking her outfit?

Of course, if it was going to make her look like a fool, that was the last thing she needed, on top of the popcorn strings and carols. She was still at the mall, technically. It wasn't too late to make an exchange.

"If you must know," she began, "this dress *isn't* mine. I was picking it up for Elizabeth. She had to have some alterations done."

"Alterations?" Janet snickered. "To add more dorky features?"

"You know, it's Elizabeth's dress, and if she wants to wear it tonight, she will," Jessica declared. She usually didn't appreciate Janet saying that Elizabeth was dorky. But she was so furious with her sister over the party plans that she didn't feel like defending her very strongly. "But I'll pass along your opinion, and maybe she'll change her mind."

"I certainly hope so," Janet said. "Isn't Elizabeth planning on taking pictures at the party for the next edition of *Sixers*? I wouldn't want the whole school to see her in that dress." She laughed.

Jessica restrained herself from punching Janet in the nose. She didn't have to make fun of her dress so relentlessly! Now what was she going to wear? "Well, if she's the one *taking* the pictures, she won't be *in* them, will she? So don't worry about it." Jessica turned to Mandy and tried to change the subject. "What are you wearing tonight?"

"Either that emerald green dress I got at the vintage shop a few weeks ago . . ." Mandy paused. "Or maybe I'll just wear a plain old red sweater, faded jeans, and my new green Doc Martens." She smiled. "Very festive."

"I'm wearing a dress," Ellen said. "But that's all I'm going to say. I think our outfits should be a surprise, like the Secret Santas."

"You know what?" Janet grinned. "I think that's exactly what we should do. But, Jessica, tell Elizabeth that if she wears that dress, she might want to disguise herself. May I suggest . . . a long white beard and a red cap?" She started laughing again. "Maybe she could even join the Witness Protection Program—the special one for fashion crimes! Come on, guys, let's hit the mall. See you tonight, Jessica!"

Jessica watched them run into the mall, giggling and laughing. Sure, they could laugh all they wanted to now. But when they saw the dress she'd pick out to replace this one, they'd be impressed—they'd even be jealous.

Jessica had obviously gotten carried away with the whole Secret Santa idea. She needed to buy something more sophisticated, to contrast with the silly carol-singing party. Something that would match her silver nail polish and earrings perfectly.

She went back into the mall to return the red dress. There it was, in the window. Fate. Looking right at her—how could she not have seen it before? A short, sleeveless, slinky, silver lamé dress!

"Danielle? I think I've changed my mind," Jessica said, walking into the store.

"Jessica, hurry up! You still need to set out the cranberries and popcorn!" Mr. Wakefield called up the stairs.

"I'll be right there!" Jessica yelled. Then she closed her bedroom door. As if she cared about cranberries and popcorn!

"Good evening, ladies and gentlemen," Jessica said into her hairbrush as she checked her reflection in the full-length mirror on the back of her bedroom door. "I'm here tonight to present the award for best evening gown in a starring role. And the Oscar goes to . . . *moi!*"

In her new silver dress, Jessica felt as glamorous as if she were going to the Academy

Awards. She twirled back and forth, watching the short hem flare around her knees. "Too bad there isn't going to be any dancing," she muttered, stepping closer to the mirror and making a last-minute adjustment to her left earring.

She checked the alarm clock beside her bed. It was nearly seven o'clock! Everyone would be showing up soon. Jessica was so excited, she nearly jumped down the stairs to the living room. But then she realized that a woman in her sort of outfit didn't rush. She strolled. Casually.

"So, is everything ready?" she asked. Her parents and Elizabeth were huddled over the table in the dining room, arranging trays of snacks and bottles of soda.

Elizabeth turned around. She was wearing a cropped green sweater over a coordinating green-and-red plaid skirt. "Is . . . is *that* what you're wearing?" she gasped.

"Yes," Jessica said, surprised. "Of course. The party's about to start, you know."

"I know," Elizabeth said. "But that dress . . ."

"It's awesome, isn't it? Just because the party has an old theme doesn't mean I can't look totally new. Watch this." Jessica spun around, giving everyone the full effect of her shimmery dress.

"Agh!" Mr. Wakefield cried as he walked into the room. He put his hands over his eyes. "What is that?"

"It's my new dress. The one I got today, thanks to Uncle Bob," Jessica said proudly.

"Uncle Bob would *not* want you to wear that dress. Trust me on this one," Mr. Wakefield said. "And I don't want you to wear it either."

"Jessica, that dress is completely inappropriate," Mrs. Wakefield said. "You can't wear that tonight. Absolutely not."

"But why not? Danielle said this dress looked great on me," Jessica said in self-defense.

Mr. Wakefield looked confused. "Who's Danielle? Boy, I can't keep track of all your friends. Is Danielle in the Unicorn Club?"

"*No*, Dad, she's the salesclerk at Valley Fashions. And she thinks—"

"Jessica, she gets paid to sell clothes. She would have told you a Santa suit looked good on you," Mrs. Wakefield said.

Actually . . . she did say that, Jessica thought. "Anyway, Danielle's not the point. The point is that this is my party and I can wear what I want!"

Steven walked into the room and burst out laughing. He tried to point at Jessica, but since he had a tray of celery and carrot sticks in his hands, he could only gesture with his elbows. He looked like a chicken. "Nice dress, Jessica. But we're going to need some of that aluminum foil later to heat up the hors d'oeuvres, so you might have to change," he said. "By the way,

did you know that 'lamé' is French for 'lame'?"
He chuckled.

Just then, the doorbell rang.

"Well, Steven? Are you going to get it or
not?" Jessica demanded, still angry about his
tinfoil comment.

Steven walked off to answer the door, shaking his head.

"Jessica, please go upstairs and change. Right
now," Mrs. Wakefield commanded. "That dress
is for someone much older than you."

"Jessica! We're here!" Lila called. "Daddy let
us use the limo so all the Unicorns could come
at once."

Jessica waved to her friends from her spot in
the dining room.

Great. They're just in time to see this! Jessica
thought, getting more and more irritated with
her mother.

"Then how come it *fits* me?" Jessica argued.

"Because it was made for a petite *woman!*"
Mrs. Wakefield practically yelled. "Now go upstairs and change into something appropriate
before the rest of your guests arrive!"

Jessica felt herself begin to blush. How could
her mother humiliate her like that, in front of
everyone? This was *her* party—if she didn't
wear her new dress, she had nothing exciting to
wear. The night would be ruined before it even
got started!

"You can borrow something of mine," Elizabeth said.

Jessica glared at her twin. *Traitor*, she thought. Couldn't Elizabeth back her up just this once? "No, thanks. I want to wear something *interesting*."

"Jessica! That's not very nice," Mrs. Wakefield said. "It's not Elizabeth's fault you're wearing that dress."

Yes, it is, Jessica thought angrily. *Because of her dumb party suggestions, I had to do something drastic to show everyone I was much cooler than this whole Christmas in 1800 idea!*

Jessica glanced at her friends, who were busy taking off their coats. They were pretending not to notice what was going on between her and her mother, but she knew that they'd heard everything. What were *they* wearing? She watched as Lila, Ellen, and Mandy draped their coats over Steven's arm until he was so overloaded, he could barely stand up.

"Come on, Jessica—get moving," Mrs. Wakefield said, nudging Jessica in the back. "You still have time to run upstairs and change before anyone else arrives."

But Jessica couldn't move. She was frozen in place in the dining room, her mouth open. Now that Janet had taken off her coat, Jessica could see what she was wearing.

A red dress with a black patent leather belt!

The very same dress Janet had told Jessica looked like a dress for Mrs. Claus!

"What a lovely dress, Janet," Mrs. Wakefield commented.

Janet looked at Jessica with a superior smile. "Thank you, Mrs. Wakefield," she said.

I would have been wearing that dress, if Janet hadn't intentionally talked me out of it, Jessica thought angrily.

Jessica felt like she was going to explode. She didn't know which was worse—being treated like a baby by her mother in front of everyone or being one-upped by Janet!

Five

◇

Jessica tossed clothes over her shoulder as she ransacked her closet. She couldn't believe Janet! She had some nerve, making fun of the dress Jessica had picked out. She'd only done that so Jessica would return the dress—then she could buy the dress and wear it herself. Some friend.

I should have listened to Danielle and kept the red dress, Jessica thought bitterly. Then she thought about the advice Danielle had given her on the silver lamé dress. Maybe Danielle wasn't to be trusted about anything!

Jessica finally pulled a cropped red fuzzy sweater out of her sweater bag and slipped it over her head. The sweater looked awesome with her short black mini, black tights, and chunky black Docs. So there! Just because she wouldn't have the best dress that night, that didn't mean she couldn't wear the hottest color of the season.

She remembered how smug Janet had looked, taking off her coat. Well, at least *Jessica's* hair didn't clash with red, the way Janet's reddish brown hair did. Jessica smiled to herself. She had looked much better in the dress.

As she went back downstairs, she was just in time to catch Ken and Aaron arriving.

"Just put your gifts under the tree, and come into the dining room for something to drink," Steven was saying.

Jessica watched Ken and Aaron place their presents on the floor. Then she stared at the accumulation of shiny wrapped gifts under the Christmas tree in the living room. Why did she have such a sinking feeling in the pit of her stomach? Why hadn't she noticed all those gifts before?

I never got Elizabeth a gift! Jessica suddenly realized, grabbing the banister to steady herself. *I'm a Secret Santa without a present!*

Everyone was going to think she was the most selfish Scrooge of the century if she didn't give out a gift. She couldn't let that happen— not with Mike coming, gift in hand, to her house, for *her* party. She'd look so rude, so thoughtless. . . . No, she absolutely could not let that happen.

The only thing she could do at this point was run back upstairs, find something to give Elizabeth, wrap it up quickly, and shove it under the tree. But she couldn't think of anything good. And a lousy gift was worse than none.

What she needed was a gift that everyone would love. Something that showed just how much she cared and what a wonderful person she could be. If only she'd made a gift, the way Elizabeth had. . . . But of course Elizabeth had had plenty of time to think about her Secret Santa gift. She hadn't spent any time being creative and coming up with original ideas for their party. She'd just sneaked behind Jessica's back and blabbered her boring old ideas to their parents, then sat back and let everything go *her* way.

When you get right down to it, Jessica thought, *Elizabeth doesn't really deserve a gift*. Elizabeth owed Jessica a favor. After all, Jessica was letting Elizabeth have her party the way she wanted.

Then Jessica had another brainstorm. One that would solve both of her problems: It would make her look good, and it would pay Elizabeth back for being a double-crosser.

She tiptoed around the tree until she located the gift with Elizabeth's handwriting on the tag. The package felt heavy and substantial. It had to be something really impressive, knowing Elizabeth.

Jessica looked over her shoulder. She could hear loud chattering in the dining room, where everyone was hanging out. Nobody would notice if she just slipped under the tree for a second and changed the tag on the gift. She pulled the tag off the gift. "To Lila, From Elizabeth," it read.

Lila? Jessica couldn't believe it. This was going to be even better than she'd hoped. Lila would get a great gift from her, and Elizabeth wouldn't get a gift. But who cared? She already had everything she wanted.

She grabbed a gift tag from the desk by the door and hastily scribbled "To Lila, From Jessica." She crumpled Elizabeth's card and stuffed it under a couch cushion. Then she secured the new card under the ribbon on the gift.

"Jessica? What are you doing?"

"Elizabeth!" Jessica stood up so suddenly, she banged her head on the branch above her. Fir needles rained down onto the presents below. "I was, uh, just, uh, putting my present under the tree," Jessica said.

"Are you *sure*?" Elizabeth asked.

Jessica didn't know what to say. Had her sister seen what she was up to? Was the whole night ruined? She held her breath, stepping out from under the tree and looking anxiously at Elizabeth.

"I think I caught you doing something else," Elizabeth said.

Jessica panicked. What was she going to say to get out of this one? "Something else? Like what?" she asked.

"I think you were just rustling around down there, looking for the gift with *your* name on it," Elizabeth continued, a teasing twinkle in her eye.

Jessica's mouth broke into a relieved smile. "OK, Elizabeth, you're right. You caught me. I was looking for mine." *Actually, I was looking for yours*, she thought. *But that's a minor detail.*

"So which one is for you?" Elizabeth asked.

"Oh, he's not here yet," Jessica said. "I mean, *it's* not down here yet. My Secret Santa must be late."

Elizabeth looked around the room. "I think everyone's here, Jessica. Well, except for Amy. Her mother's doing all this holiday baking for a community fund-raising project. She's making ten gingerbread houses, and Amy's helping."

"There's another person who isn't here yet," Jessica said. She stood up, brushing a few fir needles off her knees. "*Mike* isn't here," she whispered to Elizabeth.

"You have a crush on him, don't you?" Elizabeth asked.

"Shhh! Keep your voice down. And it's not just a crush," Jessica said under her breath. "I think he likes me too."

"Well, maybe," Elizabeth said. "But don't get your hopes up too high. You don't even know him that well yet."

"He's cute. That's all I need to know," Jessica said. "Anyway, why do you make it sound like I don't have a chance? Really, Elizabeth, you're supposed to support me a little more than that." She followed Elizabeth back into the dining room to get herself a cup of punch. All this clothes changing and gift swapping had made her incredibly thirsty.

Besides, hanging out with Elizabeth was starting to make her feel guilty. But why should she feel guilty? Elizabeth had gotten her way with everything else: the music, the food, the entertainment—and Elizabeth was always making her look bad, donating her money and clothes to charity. . . .

"Hey, Steven," Jessica said, walking over to him. "I just remembered—the party favors. Where are they?"

"I was just about to put them out," Steven said. "Don't worry, everything's under control."

"Jessica!" Mrs. Wakefield called from the kitchen. "Can you come in here, please?"

Uh-oh, Jessica thought. *The cranberry and popcorn strands!* She'd completely forgotten. She rushed into the kitchen. "Sorry, Mom. I'm right on top of it." She pulled the bags of cranberries out of the freezer.

"You didn't *defrost* them?" her mother asked.

"It'll be fine," Jessica said. "We just need a sharp needle, and I'll pop the popcorn, and—"

"I'll leave it in your hands. I've got too much to take care of," Mrs. Wakefield said, taking a pan of lasagna out of the oven.

Jessica grabbed a couple of packages of popcorn from the cupboard and tossed them into the microwave. Since you were only supposed to pop one at a time, Jessica doubled the minutes to ten. The kernels had just begun popping when Steven poked his head through the door. "Come on, Jessica. I'm handing out the party favors. And I really, really think you should be there when everyone sees the kind of ideas you had for the party."

Jessica followed him into the living room. Steven was walking around the room, carrying a giant basket filled with small gold tins. He stopped to let each party guest take one.

"These are so cute," Janet said.

"Cool! The world's smallest fruitcake!" Mandy said, grinning at Steven.

"Whose idea was this?" Lila asked. "Elizabeth's?"

"No, it was *my* idea," Jessica said proudly. "Open them up!" she urged, hoping Steven had bought some decent candy. "Everyone open their cute little boxes at the same time!"

Lila, Mandy, and Janet opened the tins. Inside were a few wrapped candies nestled on green and red tissue paper. Jessica could hardly believe it—it looked as though Steven had gone all out. "Everyone eat one!" Jessica urged. She was thrilled: The candies looked expensive, and she was sure that her friends were impressed. She looked around eagerly as her guests unwrapped their candies, then popped them into their mouths. Everyone was smiling. Jessica was proud of herself for thinking up such a wonderful, tasteful idea.

But then, something strange started happening. One by one, her friends stopped smiling. Jessica watched as Janet twisted her mouth and reached frantically for a napkin. "Ugh!" she said as she spat the candy into the napkin. "Gross! Oh, ugh, bleah, bleah, bleah!" All around Jessica, the other guests were doing the same thing.

"Ick!" cried Mandy as she reached for a cup of ginger ale. "Jessica! What have you done?"

Aaron was actually scrubbing his tongue with a napkin. "This is the most disgusting thing I've ever tasted!" he said, but since he couldn't use his tongue, it sounded like, "Thib ib the mob disgustig thig I'b eber tasteb!"

Everyone began shouting at once, except for Steven, who was doubled over with laughter, and Jessica, who was horrified. What was happening?

"Nice idea, Jessica!" Lila said angrily. "I can't wait to have *dinner!*"

"So, this is your idea of a fun party favor?" Janet demanded.

"Steven!" Jessica cried, "What have you done?"

"Hey, don't look at me," Steven said with a smirk. "Is it my fault that your guests don't like the garlic-flavored candy I bought for them at the joke shop?"

"How could you do this to me? I trusted you!" Jessica demanded, turning back to her brother.

"Hey, when you want a job done right, do it yourself," Steven said smugly, setting the empty basket back on the table. "Otherwise, take your chances!"

"You . . . you . . ." Jessica sputtered. She was so angry, she couldn't even speak.

Jessica was on the verge of tears. "I'm so sorry, everyone," she said.

"I'll bet," said Janet.

Just then, the smell of burning popcorn came wafting out of the kitchen.

"Jessica!" Mrs. Wakefield called.

Jessica was heading into the kitchen to rescue the popcorn when she heard a whining, high-pitched sound. She cringed. It sounded like a train was rolling into the living room.

Could anything else go wrong in the next five minutes? Hadn't the party gotten off to a bad enough start already?

"Is that a harmonica I hear?" Lila asked, with

a puzzled gaze toward the living room.

"Carols, everyone! Gather 'round!" Mr. Wakefield called, cupping his hands together.

Jessica raised one eyebrow. Was her dad taking nerd vitamins every morning these days, or what? She couldn't remember him ever embarrassing her so much before.

"It's my dad. He insisted on playing the harmonica," Jessica said to Lila as everyone began wandering toward the fireplace.

At least Mike isn't here to hear this, Jessica thought, glancing at the clock above the dining room table on her way into the kitchen to handle the popcorn.

"I think I'd better make another batch," Jessica said as she pulled the burned bags from the microwave.

"I'm sure some of the kernels are fine," Mrs. Wakefield said. "Put the popcorn into a bowl with the cranberries and bring them out to the living room, where everyone can help string them."

"OK." Jessica dumped the scorched popcorn over the frozen ice-ball cranberries and picked up the needle and spools of thread. *Shouldn't Elizabeth be doing this? She's the one who's into ye olde-fashioned traditional Christmas—not me!*

To her surprise, instead of being horrified by the caroling idea, all of her party guests had already gathered eagerly in front of the fireplace in a circle. Winston was seated on a chair in front of the fire, his large accordion strapped to his chest. Mr. Wakefield sat beside him, harmonica in hand.

Thank goodness Steven never took up the banjo, Jessica thought, *or I'd never hear the end of it. They'd call us the Sweet Valley Hillbillies.*

"Gross, what smells?" Lila held her nose as Jessica walked into the living room.

"It's the popcorn; it's only burned a little bit. And it's to decorate the tree, so who cares?" Jessica said, setting the bowl on the floor in the middle of the group.

"My *nostrils* care," Janet said in a snooty voice. "Jessica, don't you know how to make popcorn?"

Jessica blushed bright red. "This wasn't my idea," she told Janet.

"Just like the garlic-flavored candy wasn't *your* idea?" Janet retorted.

"All right, everyone, let's get started," Mr. Wakefield said.

"Pump it up, Egbert!" Aaron chanted. "Let's hear some accordion action!"

"You know, Mr. Wakefield, I always wanted to play the harmonica," Ken said.

"I could give you a short lesson later," Jessica's father offered.

"Sounds great!" Ken said.

Maybe this won't be so bad, after all, Jessica

thought. Nobody seemed to think it was geeky to sing along with a harmonica and an accordion. Or maybe they were just being polite, but that was OK with her too.

"So, what carol should we start with, Dad?" she asked, smiling up at him.

"How about 'Jingle Bells'?" he proposed.

"I *love* that song," Ellen said.

"Me too," Mandy added.

"Only I don't really get the 'o'er the fields we go' part. What's 'o'er' mean?" Ellen asked.

"It means they left the 'v' out of 'over,'" Mandy told her.

"Oh." Ellen giggled.

"OK, is everyone ready?" Winston asked.

Ken and Aaron hummed in harmony. "Take it away, Egbert," Ken said.

Winston and Mr. Wakefield started playing, and Jessica sang along with everyone else. "Jingle bells, jingle bells, jingle all the way . . . Oh what fun it is to ride in a one-horse open sleigh. . . ."

The doorbell rang halfway through the carol. Jessica kept singing, but she turned around so that she could see the door. When Steven pulled it open, Mike McClusky was standing on the doorstep. He pulled off his cap and handed his black corduroy coat to Steven, making small talk with him while the others continued to sing. In his hand was a small box, wrapped in red paper. *The cap!* Jessica thought excitedly. *It's the Unicorns cap for me!*

She was so excited that she didn't pay attention to the chorus—or the fact that it had just ended. She was the last one holding on to the final warbling note.

"Oh my gosh, Jessica. You sound like a sick cat!" Janet said.

Everyone started laughing. Jessica's face turned bright red.

"Come on, it wasn't that bad," Mr. Wakefield said, but he couldn't restrain from chuckling.

Jessica was appalled. Even her *dad* was laughing at her?

"Don't sweat it, Jessica. I'm just like you," Mike said as he walked up to the group. "Completely and totally tone-deaf."

"You might want to sing with the group next time," Winston said. "Your voice can sort of *blend in* that way."

Flustered, Jessica looked around the living room. She had to create a distraction. She hated being made fun of in front of a crowd. Was it her fault that she really got into singing? That the power of beautiful music overwhelmed her sometimes? Well, even if that's not what happened, whose business was it anyway?

Jessica turned to Janet. She was to blame for everyone paying so much attention to her voice in the first place. Well, two could play at this game.

But only *one* could win, and Jessica intended to be the victor.

"Well, I may not be an opera singer," she said, "but at least *I* don't look like Mrs. Claus. No, wait—*Miss* Claus." Jessica pointed at Janet's red dress and started laughing hysterically.

Nobody else joined in. Not even Mandy and Ellen, who'd laughed at *her* when she'd wanted to wear the same dress! Everyone was staring at her as if she'd just said that aliens were invading the kitchen.

"Jessica, that's not a very nice thing to say," Mr. Wakefield reprimanded her. "I think Janet looks very pretty."

"Yeah, I like that dress," Ken said with a shrug.

"Me too," Mike chimed in.

Jessica felt like crawling under the rug. She was wearing a secondhand, old-news outfit, she'd been embarrassed by her mother in front of the Unicorns, and now the carols had gotten off to a rotten start too, thanks to Janet. The party had only just started, and it was already the worst party of Jessica's life!

Six

◇

"Hi, Mike," Jessica said, trying to look casual as she moved closer to him. She had to do something to rescue the situation.

"No peeking!" Mike said, hiding his gift behind his back. He turned around and quickly slipped the box under the tree with the other gifts.

No peeking—because that's my gift, he means! Jessica thought excitedly. *Too bad for him, because I already noticed it when he came in. And I know what it is!*

"Sorry I'm so late," Mike said. "My ride got kind of messed up."

"Oh, that's OK," Jessica told him. "I'm just glad you could make it. I mean—"

"Refreshments are served!" Steven announced, standing in the doorway to the dining room.

"But we only got to sing one carol," Mandy complained.

Who cared about Christmas carols? Jessica had barely begun talking to Mike. Steven had totally interrupted their conversation! *I'm taking Steven's Christmas gift back to the store*, Jessica thought. *In fact, I'm going to take back every gift I ever gave him.*

"We'll have some more carols later—don't worry," Mr. Wakefield assured the crowd. "You'll sing even better after you've had a bite to eat."

"Then Jessica needs to eat a lot," Janet said to Lila, and the two of them cracked up all over again.

Jessica glared at Lila. Janet was bad enough, but did Lila have to join her? She was *supposed* to be Jessica's best friend. "You guys don't have to be so mean," she said.

"And you didn't have to give us disgusting candy to eat," Janet retorted.

"I told you—that was Steven's fault. Come on, Mike. Let's get some food," Jessica said, guiding him into the dining room. Jessica picked up a plate and was about to start down the buffet line.

"Jessica, please!" her mother called out in a loud voice. "Have you forgotten your manners? Guests first!"

Jessica rolled her eyes. Was she going to be embarrassed at every single turn? She might as well go upstairs to bed if this kept up. But she didn't dare. Who knows what kind of dorky antics Elizabeth and her parents would think up in her absence?

"All that so-called *singing* must have made you hungry," Janet added. "That's why you forgot."

"I didn't *forget*. I was just showing Mike and everyone, you know, where the plates are and stuff," Jessica said. She put her plate back on the stack of clean ones and stepped back from the table. "So, go ahead, help yourselves, everyone!"

She watched as her friends loaded their plates with lasagna, salad, and garlic bread. Her mouth was practically watering. By the time everyone else had gone through the line and Jessica lifted the last plate off the table, there was only one small square of lasagna left, all dried out on top and stuck to the bottom of the pan.

Why am I not surprised? Jessica thought. *The way tonight's going, I might as well have a stale piece of bread and a glass of water.* She noticed that her *sister* had a plate full of delicious-looking food.

When Jessica tried to wedge it out with a spatula, the piece of lasagna flipped into the air, narrowly missing Jessica's sweater. She managed to get her plate underneath it just before it crashed onto the carpet.

"Nice save!" Mike commented.

"Oh. Thanks." Jessica smiled faintly. She hadn't really wanted to impress Mike with her athletic coordination, but at this point, she'd take whatever she could get.

*   *   *

"Who wants to trim the tree?" Elizabeth asked, once everyone had finished eating.

"Let's do it," Mandy said, getting to her feet. "I love putting ornaments on the tree. Not to mention ribbons, popcorn chains—well, maybe not *that* popcorn." She frowned at the bowl of grayish brown scorched popcorn.

All right, already, so I burned the popcorn, Jessica thought. *Couldn't everyone just deal with it and move on?*

"Mandy once made a string of old library cards and strung them around the tree," Ellen told everyone. "It was really cool."

"That must have looked pretty funky," Mike commented. "Maybe I'll do that with our tree at home this year. My parents would have a cow, though." He laughed.

Jessica couldn't help noticing that Mike was smiling at Mandy. Jessica frowned. Mandy was stealing Jessica's spotlight. She had to do something to make sure Mike's focus stayed on her. After all, he *was* her Secret Santa. And maybe her secret admirer too.

"Hey, did you guys see this ornament?" Jessica asked, rummaging in the box until she pulled out a delicate red glass ornament with silver and gold swirls painted on it. "Mike, did you notice this one? Isn't it cool?"

"Very," Mike said. "Where did you get it?"

"Elizabeth made it. Actually, I made one just like

it, but it broke a long time ago," Jessica said. Never mind the fact that hers hadn't looked half as good: She'd gone overboard and painted the whole thing gold. She walked around the tree. "So, where should I put it?" she asked, smiling at Mike.

"Right next to that green light," Mandy said. "Then the green will light up the red glass."

Jessica turned around and glared at Mandy. *I was asking Mike!* "Do you think so? Really?" she asked Mike.

Mike shrugged. "Hey, whatever Mandy says. She's the artist."

No, Jessica thought, *she's the one who's bugging me!* She quickly slipped the hook over a tree branch. This whole tree-trimming thing wasn't nearly as much fun as she remembered. She had just turned around to pick out another ornament when she heard a loud crash behind her.

"Oh, no!" Elizabeth cried. "My favorite ornament!"

"Jessica, what did you do?" Mandy cried.

"I think she forgot to put the hook on the branch," Mike said, picking up the shattered pieces of the broken ornament.

"No, I didn't!" Jessica said. "I put it right there!" She pointed to the branch.

"Well, nobody moved the tree, and it didn't just fall off by itself," Ken commented, helping to pick up the pieces.

"You did put it on kind of fast," Lila added.

Jessica could tell she wasn't going to get

anywhere with this crowd. She might as well just give in and apologize. "I am so sorry, Elizabeth. I'll get you another one," she said.

"There isn't another one like this," Elizabeth said softly. "We made them in the first grade, remember?"

Clearly, Elizabeth wasn't going to stop until everyone thought Jessica was an insensitive jerk. Well, two could play at the "I'm so sensitive" game.

"We can make another one together," Jessica said. "It won't be exactly the same, but we can create a new memory for it, starting this year. Hey, we can make a dozen of them. Then when I'm silly enough to break another, we'll still have eleven." She smiled at her twin.

"Yeah . . . I guess," Elizabeth said, sounding completely dejected.

What does she want me to do? Crawl across the broken pieces of glass? "I know something that'll cheer you up," Jessica said, looking through the box of ornaments. "I'll put the star on top of the tree. You always love that."

Besides, it would give Jessica an opportunity to make up for breaking the ornament. She could show Mike that she really *was* as coordinated as she seemed when she was rescuing the lasagna. And how could he help but notice her when she was placing the star on top of the tree?

"OK," Elizabeth said. "Wait—let me get my camera first!" She ran into the kitchen and came back out, carrying her camera.

Jessica pulled a chair over beside the tree and climbed up, holding the shiny metal star in her right hand. "Everyone, line up in front of the tree! Ready?" she asked Elizabeth.

"Yes," Elizabeth said, lifting the camera to her eye after turning on the flash. "Come on, everyone—smile!"

Jessica leaned toward the tree, carefully starting to slip the star over the top.

"OK, Jessica. Here we go. One, two . . . ," Elizabeth chanted.

Jessica smiled at the camera, still holding on to the star, which was halfway on the tree. She took her eyes off Elizabeth for a second and glanced down at Mike to make sure he was watching her.

"Three . . ."

Jessica's legs wobbled on the chair. She was leaning too far forward, toward the tree. She was starting to lose her balance!

"Cheese!" everyone sang.

Jessica pitched forward as she slipped the star the rest of the way onto the treetop. She grabbed a branch to steady herself. She rocked back and forth on the chair, struggling to catch her balance. She shoved the tree away from her—and it tipped over!

"Look out!" she cried as the tree fell toward her friends.

Lila let out an ear-piercing shriek. *"Nooooo!"*

Seven

Mike leaped toward Lila, grabbing the tree just before it toppled onto her head.

"Man! Close call!" Ken said, helping push the tree back up so that it was standing straight.

Mike leaned over and adjusted the screws on the tree stand to hold it more firmly in place. "There. That should do it," he said, standing back up and brushing some needles off his palms. "Are you OK?" he asked Lila.

"I'm fine. Wow, I can't thank you enough. You're so *brave*," Lila said, gazing at Mike as if he were Superman.

Brave? Catching a Christmas tree? Lila's laying it on a bit thick, Jessica thought as she climbed down from the chair. *She* could have caught the tree if she wanted to.

Anyway, did anyone care that she'd nearly fallen ten feet onto the floor herself? A tree wouldn't break its bones if it fell. Nobody seemed to realize she could have been seriously injured!

"Oh, it was nothing," Mike said modestly, shrugging. "Don't worry about it."

"But I was worried," Lila protested. "When I saw that thing looming over me, about to crash onto my head . . . It was like this time I was out in the woods once, way up in Oregon, on a business trip with my father. They were cutting down gigantic trees, and this huge tree fell—right next to me!" Lila said. "I was nearly crushed!"

"Come on, Lila. That tree was, like, a mile away," Jessica reminded her. Mr. Fowler loved to tell the story of how scared Lila had been—for no reason. "And it had ropes around it, so that it was all under control."

"Still." Lila chewed her thumbnail. "It was such a huge tree that when it hit the ground, it was like the whole forest shook. Kind of a mini-earthquake. Ever since then . . . I've been afraid—"

"Of trees?" Jessica scoffed. "Get real, Lila. Who ever heard of tree phobia? It's not like you could ever really get hurt—"

"Actually, that's not true," Mike broke in. "My great-grandfather was killed by a tree."

"What?" Jessica gulped.

Mike nodded. "A tree was struck by lightning. It cracked in half and fell over, and crashed into my great-grandfather's house, which collapsed on him. He was buried in rubble."

"Oh. I'm so sorry," Jessica said. *Open mouth, insert foot.* Could she have said anything more heartless and insensitive?

"Mike, that's awful," Lila said. "I had no idea."

"Neither did I!" Jessica hurried to add.

"Nature can be a very dangerous force," Mike said. "That was kind of the lesson our family took from the whole thing."

"Yes, yes, I see." Lila put her hand on Mike's arm. "That must have been devastating."

"Actually, I never knew him." Mike shrugged. "But my mom loved him a lot."

"So, uh . . . maybe we should open the presents now!" Jessica said, trying to lighten up the mood in the room. They couldn't dwell on sad things now—it was Christmas Eve. And despite everything that had already happened to ruin her night, she was determined to salvage something from the evening.

"Good idea," Elizabeth said, smiling at her twin.

Don't smile at me, Jessica thought. *I'm the one who ought to be smiling: Lila's about to receive a gift from the greatest friend in the world—me!* "How do you want to do this?"

"I'll hand out the gifts, one by one," Elizabeth volunteered. "OK with everyone?"

"Sounds good," Aaron said, taking a seat on the carpet.

Everyone sat down in a giant circle, and

Elizabeth pulled the first gift out from under the tree. "Oh, wait—Amy's not here yet. I hate to start without her," Elizabeth said.

"I bet she'll come in halfway through," Maria Slater said. "She thought she'd be done helping her mother right around now."

"OK. Then I'll start," Elizabeth said. "Let's see . . . this one is for Ken." She handed a large, flat box to Ken.

"To Ken, From Aaron." He unwrapped it quickly and pulled out a Sweet Valley High football team T-shirt. "Property of SVH Athletic Department," Ken read, nodding and smiling. "Awesome!"

"I'm sure you'll be on the team someday, so I thought you should start getting used to the school colors," Aaron told him.

"Thanks. This is great," Ken said with a grin.

"Next up." Elizabeth grabbed a tiny box. "For Mandy, From Ken." She handed the box to Mandy. "Hmmm . . . I wonder what that could be."

Mandy started tearing off the wrapping paper. "How did you know, Ken? Diamonds are a girl's best friend!"

"Yeah, and they're also a little over ten dollars," Ken said, laughing. "Sorry."

Everyone laughed.

"OK, then, what is it?" Mandy lifted the lid off the small box and pulled out a key chain. A funky black shoe just like the ones Mandy always wore dangled from the chain. "This is so cool! Thanks, Ken."

"You're welcome," he said, looking embarrassed. "I would have bought you the matching shoes too, but—"

"They're over ten dollars. Yeah, yeah, Ken, I know. Spare me the excuses, OK?" Mandy teased him. "Seriously, thanks. I'll put all my keys on here right now, and get rid of my tacky Las Vegas key chain I got when I was eight."

"That thing. I've been hoping you'd get rid of that for years," Lila said, flipping her hair over her shoulder.

"I know," Mandy said. "Remember the time you tried to throw it out, accidentally-on-purpose— with the keys still on it?"

"Who, *moi?*" Lila said, putting her hand over her heart.

"And now for present number three," Elizabeth said, reaching for another box under the tree. "This one's for Jessica! How exciting!"

Jessica's heart started beating faster.

"And it's from . . . ," Elizabeth went on. *I know who it's from,* Jessica thought. She turned to Mike with a gracious smile.

"Winston Egbert!"

Jessica coughed. *"Winston?"*

Winston nodded proudly. "And I hope you'll have as much fun opening it as I did wrapping it."

I doubt it, Jessica thought. Stupid Winston.

Didn't he know that Mike was supposed to be her Secret Santa? Poor Mike must be so disappointed! What did Winston know about what she liked or what she didn't like? Jessica took off the wrapping paper and opened the box. Inside was another box. And another box. "Is this a trick?" Jessica muttered, struggling to unwrap them as quickly as she could. She couldn't imagine what was so small as to be hidden in the last tiny box. Finally, Jessica pulled a thin gold piece of paper out of the smallest box. It was scrolled up and had a ribbon around it. "Excellent! A gift certificate!" she said.

"A very personal gift certificate," Winston said, sounding a bit mischievous.

Jessica unrolled the paper. Pasted in the center of the paper was a square green piece of construction paper, cut into the shape of an accordion. "This entitles you to three accordion lessons at the House of Egbert Music Hall. Retail value: $10. You'll be playing polkas in no time!" Jessica tried to smile. "Accordion lessons. How . . . nice."

"I thought you might want to learn how to play, so you and your dad could play duets next year," Winston said. "Of course, you could always trade in the accordion lessons for something else."

"I could?" Jessica asked eagerly.

"Sure. For instance, a singing lesson," Winston said.

Everyone started laughing.

Jessica stuffed the so-called gift certificate back

into its box. Great. Not only did he give her a lousy, useless gift, he was going to make fun of her again too. Who invited Winston anyway? "Isn't it time for somebody to open another gift?" she asked.

"Sure," Elizabeth said with a sympathetic glance toward Jessica. "How about this one?" Jessica stared as Elizabeth picked up a box and read off, "For Ellen, From Mike."

Ellen? Since when did she deserve to have Mike as her Secret Santa? She barely even knew he was alive!

Ellen tore open the package and pulled out a purple baseball cap. "The Utah Unicorns! Awesome! How did you know I liked basketball?" She grinned at Mike.

Because of me! Jessica thought, furious. *Because he asked me stuff about me and my friends—trying to get information about you!* This wasn't fair! Nothing was working out the way it was supposed to.

"And now for the final Secret Santa gift," Elizabeth said about ten minutes later. "And I think I saved the best for last—or at least the heaviest. No offense to anyone."

"Oh, fine, Elizabeth. *Knock* my accordion lessons," Winston said, pretending to be highly insulted. "See if they let you into the Polka Hall of Fame now."

"Like you'll get in," Aaron teased him.

"Hey, for the three-fifty admission fee, anything's possible," Winston replied with a chuckle.

Jessica fidgeted nervously with a loose piece of carpet pile. Here it came. The moment of truth. *You'd better back me up on this, Elizabeth,* she thought. *After all, you got to have the party exactly the way you wanted it. Nothing's worked out for me tonight. Steven sabotaged my party favors. I burned the popcorn and froze the cranberries. You owe me a favor!*

"This is for Lila," Elizabeth said, handing her present to Mandy, who passed it to Ellen, who gave it to Lila.

"I was starting to think I wasn't going to get anything," Lila said.

"Hey, wait a second. Is that all the presents there are?" Mike asked.

"Why, did you want another?" Ken teased him.

"No, not for *me*. Elizabeth didn't get one." Mike pointed to the empty space in front of Elizabeth. "Is somebody sick?"

"No, everybody's here," Mandy said. "Except for Amy, who should be here any second. And that gift on the coffee table is for her."

"She already gave me my present," Aaron said. "She left the present with Elizabeth, remember?"

"Well then . . . who was supposed to get Elizabeth a gift?" Mike asked.

Jessica's stomach turned over. Being smart was nice and all, but did he have to be so *observant*? "So, Lila, open your present," she urged. Out of the corner of her eye, she saw Elizabeth looking around the bottom of the tree, as if she might find her gift there. *Not very likely,* Jessica thought. *Unless the real Santa Claus sneaked in here when we weren't looking.*

"Maybe I forgot to put my name in the hat the other day," Elizabeth mused. "Or maybe it got stuck to someone else's slip of paper and fell out."

"Yeah, I bet that's what happened," Jessica said quickly. *Hey, why didn't I think of that excuse earlier?*

Lila tore off the wrapping paper and pulled out the photo album. "Lila's Yearbook," she read out loud. "Cool!" She flipped through the first few pages, admiring the photographs and laughing at the captions. "This is so awesome!"

She showed the album to Janet and Mandy, who were sitting beside her. "Look at all these pictures of me—and us. It's so thoughtful. Who made this? It must have taken hours! Who gave this to me?" Lila asked.

"Read the tag!" Elizabeth said excitedly.

Jessica crossed her fingers. *Please don't ruin this for me, Elizabeth. I'm having such a rotten time at this party as it is—it can't get worse!* "Yeah, Lila, find the tag," she urged.

Lila rustled through the crumpled ball of wrapping paper. "To Lila, From Jessica," she read out loud. "I should have known! Only Jessica knows me this well." She beamed a smile across the circle at Jessica.

"J-Jessica?" Elizabeth sputtered.

Jessica felt a lump in her throat as she stared at Elizabeth's quivering lip. Maybe she shouldn't have done that. *But Elizabeth deserved it!* Jessica thought. *I'm glad she's unhappy. Now she knows how it feels to have things turn out wrong.*

The doorbell rang. Steven was sitting by the door, and he hopped up to answer it. "Hey, Amy!" he said. "Come on in."

Amy rushed into the house, tossing her jacket onto a chair. "Oh, no! Did I miss everything?" She looked around the circle. "Wow, you opened all your gifts already. Hey, Lila," she said, taking an empty spot beside her as she sat down. She pointed to the gift in Lila's hands. "What did you think of that photo album Elizabeth made for you? Isn't it incredible?"

"*Elizabeth* made this for me?" Lila asked.

"Yeah, I happened to bust in on her when she was working on it, so she had to tell me it was for you," Amy admitted. "Kind of blew the whole Secret Santa thing, but I didn't tell anyone else."

"But I thought—wait a second. Which one of you guys gave this to me?" Lila asked, staring at Elizabeth, then at Jessica. "You, or you?"

Jessica hummed to herself as she fidgeted with Winston's gift certificate. *Remain calm. It's not over yet. However, it is getting close. You might want to check the exits.*

"Elizabeth, obviously," Amy said. "Check the inscription at the beginning."

Jessica's eyes opened wide. Inscription? What inscription?

Lila flipped to the front of her yearbook. "It says right here, in Elizabeth's handwriting: To Lila, Happy Christmas Memories from Elizabeth." Lila put the photo album on the floor and stared at Jessica. "You stole this gift from Elizabeth! You tried to pass it off as your own!"

"I . . . no, I didn't," Jessica fumbled for words.

"You didn't give anyone a gift?" Aaron uttered, stunned.

"You didn't buy anything, did you?" Janet asked.

Winston shuddered. "You had to take Elizabeth's and pretend it was yours, because you didn't buy a gift. And you figured she'd be too nice to turn you in."

"Which she is," Amy said angrily. "But guess what, Jessica. *We're* not! We know exactly what you did."

Jessica felt like the prime suspect in a mystery movie, when the detective gathered everyone into a room to read out her findings.

"I can't believe you," Lila said. "Pretending to give me a present like that. Who were you supposed to buy a present for anyway?"

"Yeah, who didn't get to have a Secret Santa?" Mike asked. His eyebrows disappeared under his bangs as he realized the truth. "Oh my gosh. Elizabeth."

Everyone started getting to their feet, casting disappointed, disgusted looks at Jessica.

Lila rushed across the circle and wrapped her

arms around Elizabeth, hugging her tightly. "This is so typical! She had to hog the spotlight, when you're the one who really deserves it."

"You're in the spotlight now, Jessica," Janet said. "But probably not the way you wanted."

"It was a . . . a mistake!" Jessica said. "It could have happened to anybody!"

"Yeah, anybody who doesn't have a *heart*," Ellen said.

"You know those accordion lessons I offered you?" Winston snatched the box out of Jessica's hands and ripped the certificate into a dozen pieces. "Forget it. You don't deserve to get anywhere near such a beautiful instrument."

"If Santa Claus really does keep a list, you're on the bad one," Aaron chided.

"Yeah, the one titled 'Creeps,'" Mandy added.

"Look up 'Christmas' in the dictionary, Jessica, the next time you think about stealing someone's gift," Ken said.

Jessica had never had so many insults hurled her way at once. She felt like a small island under enemy attack. "I didn't mean—" she began to explain. "I wasn't trying to—"

"Go ahead. Explain your way out of this one. But don't expect us to be here when you finish," Ellen said.

Jessica felt a tear trickle down her cheek. Ellen, who never had a mean word to say about anyone? Even Ellen hated her now?

"Elizabeth, do you want to come stay at *my* house tonight?" Lila offered. "You might want to bring all your gifts too, so Jessica doesn't take them and give them away as her own."

Mike came over to Jessica, holding his coat. "I know I haven't known you very long, Jessica. But already, I have this feeling . . ."

Jessica's heart started pounding faster. Maybe her trick hadn't bothered Mike as much as it bugged everyone else! "A feeling?" she asked timidly, wiping a tear off her cheek.

"Yeah. A feeling that we're *never* going to be friends," Mike continued. "Not after what you did to Elizabeth tonight. Good night, and good riddance." He threw his coat over his shoulder and marched out the door.

"I don't care what any of you think," Jessica said bitterly. "I hate all of you!"

She ran upstairs and slammed the door to her bedroom. Then she collapsed on her bed and burst into tears. Why did things have to turn out that way? "I wish this day had never happened!" she sobbed into her pillow. "I wish this Christmas Eve didn't exist!"

Eight

◇

Jessica stretched her arms over her head and rolled over in bed, staring up at the ceiling. A car outside honked its horn, and Jessica frowned. Who would honk their horn on Christmas morning? Christmas Eve was in poor enough taste, Jessica thought. But Christmas morning too? *We must have some new, really obnoxious neighbors.*

Wait a second. It's Christmas!

Jessica tossed off the covers and climbed out of bed. From the bathroom in between her and Elizabeth's rooms, she heard the shower knobs squeak as Elizabeth turned off the water. *Why is Elizabeth taking a shower before we open our presents? She usually runs in, jumps on my bed, and we rush downstairs before we do anything else.*

Suddenly, her stomach gave a sickening lurch as

Jessica remembered what had happened the night before. She'd ruined the party by stealing Elizabeth's gift. Everyone hated her. Including Elizabeth.

But the flash of guilt was gone in a second. *Well, good,* she thought. *I hope she is upset. But why should she be? I'm the one who had the terrible evening.*

Jessica was dreading the inevitable lecture her parents would give her over breakfast. This was probably going to be the worst Christmas she'd ever had. Jessica sighed. Well, there was nothing much she could do about it now. She might as well go downstairs and get it over with, so she could just apologize and they could start opening their presents. That is, if anyone was going to give her any presents. If they hadn't returned them all to the stores already.

I don't care if they're mad at me. I'm mad at all of them too, Jessica thought. She had plenty of things to be mad about. How about the way Elizabeth and her parents got together and planned the party behind Jessica's back? How about Steven turning her party-favor idea into a practical joke? She wasn't to blame for everything.

As Jessica quickly changed from her flannel pajamas into a pair of jeans and a sweater, she heard her parents walk by in the hallway, on their way downstairs.

"Well, I don't know if we should give the kids his cards this morning or tomorrow morning." It was her mother's voice.

"Bob wants them to open the cards on Christmas Eve. There's really no point in waiting until tomorrow," her father replied.

What are they talking about? Jessica wondered as she slid her feet into a pair of brown suede clogs. *It's Christmas Day! They already gave us our cards from Uncle Bob yesterday. That's how I bought that dress. That stupid, ugly silver dress.* She couldn't wait to return it. She wanted a *full* refund. And an apology from Danielle.

Jessica opened her bedroom door and walked downstairs to the kitchen. Steven and Elizabeth were already seated at the breakfast table. "Good . . . morning," she said cautiously, with a nervous smile at her twin.

"Good morning, Jessica," Mrs. Wakefield greeted her warmly.

"Hi there." Mr. Wakefield slid into a seat opposite Steven and opened the morning newspaper to the business section.

This was a little creepy. Everyone was acting normal. Too normal. *Why aren't they yelling at me?* Jessica wondered. *Because it's Christmas?*

And why is everyone eating breakfast instead of rushing to open presents? Maybe they're just trying to build up the suspense so that I break down and apologize. Well, I won't do it. I'll apologize to them when they apologize to me.

I'll just play along, Jessica thought. She sat down at the table and braced herself.

Steven looked at her over the top of the sports section. "What happened to you?"

Wasn't it obvious? Jessica thought. "What do you mean?" she asked cautiously.

"I think you should go back to bed," Steven said. "You could use a few more hours' worth of beauty sleep."

Wait a second, Jessica thought. *Didn't we have this conversation yesterday?* "If you're going to insult me, you could at least think up some new material," Jessica told him.

"Huh?" Steven said, looking confused.

"You said that to me yesterday morning at breakfast," Jessica said. "Remember?"

"No. We didn't eat breakfast together yesterday morning," Steven said. "I had breakfast with Elizabeth."

"No, you didn't," Jessica said. "I was right here!"

"You definitely need to sleep more," Steven commented. "You're losing touch with reality."

Right back at you, Jessica thought.

"You kids go ahead and get all your arguments out of the way now," Mr. Wakefield said, calmly shaking out the newspaper as he turned the page. "Then we won't have any problems tonight."

"The last thing you want to do is argue in front of your guests," Mrs. Wakefield added helpfully.

Guests? Jessica wondered, stopping with her glass of orange juice halfway to her lips. What guests were they having over Christmas night? They usually spent the whole day together, just family.

"Don't worry Mom. When everyone shows up, I'll be cool, I promise." Steven said. "But next time I have a party, I want Jessica and Elizabeth to help out."

"No problem," Elizabeth told him, smiling.

Holiday party? But they'd already had their party. Was everyone in denial because it had been so awful? If anyone wanted to forget it, that person was Jessica. But she knew it had happened, as clearly as she knew that they were eating cold cereal on Christmas morning.

Wait a second! We never eat cold cereal on Christmas! Mom always bakes a special cinnamon coffee cake, Dad cooks bacon, and we flip a coin to see who makes the eggs!

Jessica looked nervously around the kitchen. Had everyone in her family gone insane? Or—she gulped down a spoonful of cereal—maybe *she* had gone insane.

So was it Christmas or wasn't it? *Maybe—maybe yesterday was only a dream!* Jessica thought, growing excited. *That's it: I dreamed the whole thing. It was just a horrible, incredibly long, and utterly realistic nightmare!*

But Jessica's relief was short-lived. *Wait a minute,* she thought. *Then why is everything happening exactly the same way that it happened in my dream? Am*

I psychic? Or am I reliving the same day over again?
This was starting to make Jessica even more uncomfortable than the thought that her parents
might yell at her had.

This is just some elaborate coincidence! Jessica tried
to comfort herself. *My imagination really went wild
for a minute there.*

Jessica decided she would try a little test.
When she saw the results, she'd know whether
she was reliving history. "Mom, Dad? Do you
think I could borrow a little money? I really need
a new dress to wear to the *party* tonight." She
looked around the table. Nobody jumped up and
protested, "What party!" or, "It's Christmas;
nothing will be open!" Jessica felt a prickle on the
back of her neck.

"You're buying a new dress?" Elizabeth asked.
"I'm not. In fact, I think I have too many clothes.
Last night, I was building up a huge collection of
clothes I don't wear or that don't fit anymore, to
give away to charity. Do you have some to add?"

"N-No," Jessica stammered. She didn't know
what to say, so she just said what came to her automatically. "I need all of them."

"Well, Sweet Valley Home Services is having
a special clothing drive, because of the holidays," Elizabeth said. "So if you come across
anything . . ."

"I . . . won't," Jessica said. She turned back to her
parents. "So what do you say, Mom and Dad? Can

you advance me a little on my January allowance?"
As if I don't know what their answer to that will be.

"No," Mr. Wakefield said.

"Not a chance," Mrs. Wakefield added.

That's exactly what they'd said yesterday, Jessica realized.

"However, your uncle Bob might be able to help you out." Mr. Wakefield slid an envelope across the table to Jessica, and then gave one each to Elizabeth and Steven.

Did this mean Jessica was going to have another fifty-dollar check? So that now she'd have one hundred dollars? But if yesterday had truly never happened, then she wouldn't have gotten the first check. And she wouldn't have bought the silver dress. Or made any of those other mistakes.

Does this mean what I think it means? That my wish last night came true? That yesterday never really happened, and I'm getting a second chance?

Before she opened her card from Uncle Bob, Jessica grabbed a section of the newspaper. "December 24" was written at the top. It was true: It was Christmas Eve all over again!

Jessica grinned, tearing open the envelope. She took out the check and lifted it to her lips. "Thank you, Uncle Bob! I'll look gorgeous tonight, thanks to you."

"Wow, how generous. I think I'll add this to my donation to the clothing drive," Elizabeth said.

"I'll be happy to drive you and your stuff over

there later today," Mrs. Wakefield said. "But first, I think we ought to bake some more cookies for the party tonight. I'm afraid we don't have nearly enough."

"Oh, OK," Elizabeth said. "That'll be fun. You can help, right, Jessica?"

Jessica's mind was whirling with all of the things she had to accomplish that day.

"Um—what? Cookies? No . . . no, I—I have to go to the mall," she said. "I have more shopping to do. You know—presents. For my Secret Santa gift."

"And for yourself," Steven mumbled.

"Maybe you could go to the mall this after-noon," Mrs. Wakefield suggested. "We could really use your help in the kitchen."

"But the stores are going to close early, because it's Christmas Eve," Jessica said. "Sorry!" She de-cided to skip the rest of this discussion—she knew exactly where it was headed. A second chance! She couldn't believe it. She had so much to do! "Don't worry, I'll be home just as soon as I find the perfect dress," Jessica promised. It wouldn't take much time, now that she knew which dress to buy—and keep—no matter what Janet said. She wouldn't let Janet sabotage her outfit again. *Speaking of sabotage . . . that reminds me of another little problem I have to take care of.*

"Oh, Steven. You know how you were going to help me with the party favors?" she asked. "Don't worry about it. I'll take care of everything."

His face fell. "Are you sure? I really wanted to help."

I bet! Help embarrass me, you mean! "I really appreciate the offer, but this is something I'd rather do myself," she told him with a sweet smile. She dug into her cereal. "Boy, is this breakfast delicious!"

"So, Elizabeth. You're sure you still want to have that old-fashioned junk tonight?" Jessica asked as she cleared the breakfast table.

"Of course. It's all been decided," Elizabeth said.

"And you won't even consider changing anything? No matter what?" Jessica said.

"What do you mean?" Elizabeth turned around from the sink, a puzzled expression on her face.

"The party. It's going to be the way you planned," Jessica said.

"Look, Jessica, I know you had lots of ideas for the party, but I just don't think they're practical," Elizabeth said.

They may not be practical, but at least they're not boring, Jessica thought, raising an eyebrow. "Fine. Then the party will be just the way you like." *She can't say I didn't give her a chance to change her mind.* Having the party the way Elizabeth wanted just meant there were certain consequences. And now that Jessica knew what was going to happen, she could make sure that "Operation Get Back at Elizabeth" went smoothly.

Jessica thought back over the previous night. Where had she gone wrong? First there was the inscription, and then there was the poorly timed arrival of Amy Sutton. *Anytime Amy shows up is the wrong time,* Jessica thought. But first things first.

She quietly went into the den, where all the gift wrap was stored. She took a large, square gold-foil sticker off the roll of gift labels. Then she sneaked upstairs to her sister's room.

She found the present on Elizabeth's desk, in plain sight. The photo album was already wrapped and ready to go. Jessica carefully removed the Scotch tape on one end and slid the album out. She opened to the front page, where Elizabeth had inscribed the photo album, "To Lila, Happy Christmas Memories from Elizabeth."

Jessica took the gold-foil sticker out of her pocket. She peeled off the back and pasted it right on top of the inscription. It fit perfectly. Then she took a green pen from the cup on Elizabeth's desk and wrote on the sticker: "To Lila, Merry Christmas! Love, Jessica." There! Lila would never know that the gift was originally from Elizabeth now. Jessica would look like the best gift giver in the world, and Elizabeth would get just what she deserved. *If you're going to go behind my back and ruin the party for me,* she thought, *then I'm going to go behind your back and ruin the party for you.*

She carefully rewrapped the gift and covered the new gift tag with curling ribbon. Elizabeth would never suspect a thing . . . until it was too late.

Now, to keep Amy away from the party. She'd been late because she was helping bake gingerbread houses. How could she use that to her advantage?

Jessica walked back to the kitchen. "Elizabeth, who did you say Amy and her mother were doing all that baking for?"

"It's called Sweet Valley Neighbors and Friends. Why?" Elizabeth asked, rinsing a plate.

"Oh, I thought I might, you know, volunteer," Jessica said. *Volunteer to make twice as much work for Amy, that is!* She went back into the den and picked up the telephone, dialing Amy's number.

"Hello?" Mrs. Sutton answered the phone.

Jessica pinched her nose to disguise her voice. "Hello, Mrs. Sutton. This is Andrea, down at Sweet Valley Neighbors and Friends. How's the baking going?"

"Fine. Do I know you?" Mrs. Sutton asked.

"No, we haven't met. I work the early-morning shift. Listen, we've just gotten a request for ten more gingerbread houses. Do you think you could get those ready for tomorrow?"

"T-T-Ten? By tomorrow?" Mrs. Sutton sounded faint.

"I know it's a lot of work. But we have a, uh, a company. With lots of money to spend. And they want to give one house each to every, er, employee," Jessica said. "This would raise lots of money for our group. For our families. For our city."

"Yes, I see. Well, I'll try my best," Mrs. Sutton said. "My daughter and I may be up all night, but—"

"But isn't that what Christmas is all about? Thank you!" Jessica hung up the phone, propping her feet on the desk. Everything was all falling into place for *Christmas Eve, Part Two: Jessica's Revenge!*

"That red dress looks adorable on you," Danielle told Jessica when she came out of the dressing room at Valley Fashions later that morning. "I love that belt."

Jessica stared at Danielle's reflection in the mirror. *I don't care what you think!* she thought. *All that matters is what I think. And this is the dress I want.* "I'll take it," Jessica declared. "You said thirty percent off, right?" That was one part of the day Jessica *didn't* want to change.

Danielle nodded. "Yes, it's our special last-minute sale. You've got perfect timing," Danielle said.

"I certainly do," Jessica said proudly. Especially when it comes to the second time around!

Wait until Mike saw her in that dress. He'd forget all about her bad singing, and Janet's jokes, and Mandy's artistry. All he'd be able to see was *her.*

"Jessica! Hi!" Mandy said.

"Hey, Mandy," Jessica said, stopping as she

was halfway out the door of the mall. *Well, what do you know.* Mandy, Ellen, and Janet had shown up, just like clockwork. But this time, Jessica was ready for them. Just let Janet try to insult her. *This ought to be fun.*

"Wow, I thought you'd be home all day getting ready for the party," Mandy commented.

"I'm going there now," Jessica said, looking at Ellen and Janet. So far, everything was going exactly as it had the day before. Only, she wasn't going to make the same mistake. In fact, she couldn't wait to see Janet's face when she told her she wasn't going to return the red dress. Not now that she knew what Janet was up to!

"You guys are going to have a great time tonight," Jessica told them. "It's not going to be exactly how I wanted it, but you know how it is. Parents. Sisters. Brothers." She wrinkled her nose to show her displeasure.

"Don't worry, Jessica, we'll make the best of it," Janet said, rolling her eyes. "As long as all the Unicorns are there, it's automatically a good time. So, what did you buy?" Janet asked. "Your Secret Santa gift?"

"No," Jessica said. *Spare me,* she thought. *The person I'm Secret Santa for is going to get just what she deserves. And I hope Janet buys that silver lamé dress— let her see how it feels to be laughed at!* "Check this out." Jessica took the red dress out of the bag and held it up against her body.

"Wow, that's . . . cute!" Ellen said.

"Definitely a holiday party dress," Mandy said, nodding.

Jessica looked at Janet, who was once again staring at the dress with a disgusted expression.

"Are you going to wear black patent leather boots and a big white beard too?" she said scornfully.

"I don't know what you're talking about," Jessica said smugly.

"No, wait—I get it!" Janet cried, fingering the dress material. "This isn't a man's outfit. Oh, no. It's the dress that *Mrs*. Claus wears every Christmas Eve."

"Actually, *your* outfit looks more like Mrs. Claus," Jessica said, pointing at Janet's big red puffy jacket. "You could really get a lot of use out of that at the North Pole. Of course, in California, you just look sort of overdressed."

Ellen giggled. "That jacket is sort of huge. Is that a ski jacket?"

"Or a water-ski jacket?" Mandy asked. "It looks waterproof."

"It looks *everything*-proof." Jessica smiled with satisfaction. It felt much better to be on the giving end of insults than the receiving end.

"I still say her dress looks like a Santa Claus uniform," Janet said in a grumpy tone.

"Oh, Janet. Don't be so *Claus*trophobic," Jessica said as Mandy and Ellen cracked up. Jessica carefully folded the dress and put it back in the bag. "I wanted something extra-special for tonight."

"It's special, all right," Janet said. "Especially ugly!" She laughed. "I hope Elizabeth doesn't take any pictures tonight for *Sixers*. I wouldn't want everyone at school to make fun of you!"

This is amazing. Even though I know what she's up to, I still want to punch Janet in the nose, Jessica thought.

"You guys, come on. It's Christmas! Quit arguing," Mandy said.

"You're right," Jessica said, crossing her fingers behind her back. "I'm sorry, Janet. I didn't mean to make fun of your jacket."

"And I'm sure I didn't mean to laugh at your dress," Janet said, smiling sweetly.

Jessica knew Janet was lying through her teeth. But Jessica was lying too, so she didn't really care. "Have fun shopping, you guys. See you tonight!" she said, turning to walk away.

She wished she could be a fly on the wall when Janet went to Valley Fashions—and found the dress she wanted *wasn't there!*

Nine

◇

"Jessica! What a lovely dress," Mrs. Wakefield said when Jessica came downstairs at seven o'clock to greet her first guests that evening.

"Thanks, Mom," Jessica said. "Do you think it's . . . appropriate?"

"Very appropriate," her mother told her, smiling. "You couldn't have chosen a nicer one."

"That's what I thought too. And Danielle agreed with me," Jessica said.

"Who's Danielle?" Mr. Wakefield asked. "I can't keep track of your friends. Is she in the Unicorn Club?"

"No, Dad. She's a salesclerk at the mall." *But if I spend any more time with her, she might become one of my friends,* Jessica thought, resisting the urge to giggle.

Just then, the doorbell rang. "Well, are you

going to get it or not?" Jessica asked Steven.

"But of course, madam." He walked off to answer the door, shaking his head.

"Jessica! We're here!" Lila called, striding through the front door. "Daddy let us use the limo so all the Unicorns could come at once."

"Hey, you guys!" Jessica replied. She glanced at her friends, who were busy taking off their coats. She watched as Lila, Ellen, Mandy, and the other Unicorns draped their coats over Steven's arm until he was so overloaded, he could barely stand up.

Jessica grinned. Janet was wearing a green jumper over a white turtleneck. If there was a more plain and boring outfit in the world, Jessica couldn't think of it.

"What a pretty dress," Mary Wallace said, admiring Jessica.

"Thanks, Mary." This time, it was Jessica who looked at Janet with a superior smile. "Red is the color of the season, isn't it? I heard they sold out of it at the mall." She restrained herself from leaping up and down and shouting, "Victory!" That would be gloating.

"Is that a harmonica I hear?" Lila asked with a puzzled gaze toward the living room.

"Carols, everyone! Gather 'round!" Mr. Wakefield called, cupping his hands together.

There were a lot of advantages to this "living the day over again" approach, Jessica decided as she wandered into the living room carrying a bowl of perfectly popped popcorn and defrosted cranberries. She didn't smell like scorched carpet, and she already knew that she didn't have to be embarrassed by her dad. Steven hadn't gotten to play his practical joke. All she had to watch out for was her singing. But she had a plan for how to overcome that little problem.

Jessica glanced at the clock above the dining room table on her way out of the room. Mike would be there any minute, and his timing was going to be perfect.

Winston was seated on a chair in front of the fire, his large accordion strapped to his chest. Mr. Wakefield sat beside him, harmonica in hand.

"Pump it up, Egbert!" Aaron chanted. "Let's hear some accordion action!"

"You know, Mr. Wakefield, I always wanted to play the harmonica," Ken said.

"I could give you a short lesson later," Jessica's father offered.

I wish I could fast-forward through all of the boring parts of this day, Jessica thought.

"Sounds great!" Ken said.

"So, what carol should we start with, Dad?" Jessica asked, smiling up at him. *As if I don't know the answer.*

"How about 'Jingle Bells'?" he proposed.

"I *love* that song," Ellen said.

"Me too," Mandy added.

"Only I don't really get the 'o'er the fields we go' part. What's 'o'er' mean?" Ellen asked.

Jessica tugged on Janet's sleeve. "Can I ask you a favor?"

"What is it?" Janet asked.

"Well, this is kind of embarrassing. But 'Jingle Bells' is my dad's favorite song in the whole entire world," Jessica said. "That's why he wants to start with it. And he always insists on me singing it really loudly and drawing out the last notes, because he likes the way I sing."

"He does?" Janet raised her eyebrows.

"Yes. You know how parents are," Jessica said. "And it's OK, when it's just my family. But I'll be really embarrassed if I have to do it on my own, in front of everyone. And you have such a beautiful voice, Janet. Do you think you could sing with me?"

"Well . . . I guess I could," Janet said. She cleared her throat. "I do have the best soprano voice in the eighth grade."

"Exactly," Jessica said. "That's exactly what I need."

"Sure, I'll do it," Janet agreed.

"Thanks. This *really* means a lot to me," Jessica told her. *You have no idea how much! Or how much it's going to mean to everyone else too. . . .*

"OK, is everyone ready?" Winston asked.

Ken and Aaron hummed in harmony. "Take it away, Egbert," Ken said.

Winston and Mr. Wakefield started playing, and Jessica sang along with everyone else.

"Jingle bells, jingle bells, jingle all the way. Oh what fun it is to ride in a one-horse open sleigh. . . ."

"Jessica, are you singing? I can hardly hear you," her father whispered.

"I'm just trying to harmonize," Jessica said. She turned to Janet as if to say, "See? I told you he likes it when I sing this song really loud." But when she turned away from Janet, she kept her voice at an almost inaudible level. She wasn't going to fall into the trap of belting out the lyrics again. She'd let someone *else* hog the spotlight tonight. Namely, Janet. Which would serve her right for the dirty trick she had pulled the day before.

The doorbell rang, and Mike walked into the living room, taking off his coat. Jessica only mouthed the lyrics from that point on.

Without her voice, the chorus sort of died out—except for Janet, who held the ending note, the way Jessica had asked her to.

"Jessica, what happened to you? We were supposed to be singing that part *together*," Janet said.

"I know, and I'm sorry, but I couldn't harmonize with you, because you sound like a sick cat!" Jessica said with a giggle. She waited for everyone to start laughing, the way they had at her.

Instead, blank faces greeted her everywhere she turned. All the faces but Janet's, that is, who looked like she was about to cry. Finally, somebody spoke.

"Don't worry about it, Janet. I can't always get into perfect harmony when I'm singing Christmas carols either," Mike said.

Janet smiled at him. "Thanks." She shot Jessica an evil look.

Wait a second, Jessica thought. *Janet and Mike are not supposed to* bond *over bad singing! If anyone's supposed to do that, it's me and Mike—we're the ones who are tone-deaf. He said so himself last time!*

"And everyone should participate—*that's* what really matters," Mike continued, as if he'd noticed that Jessica hadn't sung the final two refrains.

Jessica cleared her throat nervously. "Actually, what I meant was, *I* felt like a sick cat. That's why I wasn't singing. Scratchy throat." She rubbed her neck vigorously. "You know, like when a cat swallows too much fur and gets a hair ball—"

"Forget it, Jessica." Janet shook her head. "We *heard* what you really said."

Mike just looked at Jessica with a strange expression on his face.

Don't panic, Jessica told herself. *There's still plenty of time to recover.* "You guys misunderstood. Really," she insisted.

"Refreshments are served!" Steven called from the dining room.

Saved by Steven! I never would have imagined. Now I can escape from this mess, Jessica thought. She practically ran over to the buffet table. Then she stopped, remembering her mistake from the night before.

"Go ahead, Jessica," Steven said, handing her a plate from the stack.

"Oh, no. I couldn't," she said, stepping back.

"Don't you know the first rule of hosting a party? The hostess always has to eat first. No one can even pick up a fork until you do," Steven whispered.

"Is that true?" Jessica asked.

"I was reading this etiquette book this afternoon—trying to learn how to be a good waiter. There was an entire *section* on how the hostess has to start the buffet line," Steven said. "And the first dance too."

"Oh. Well, OK." Jessica picked up a plate and started to help herself to lasagna.

"Jessica, please! Have you forgotten your manners? Guests first!" her mother called over the din of conversation.

"*Really,* Jessica," Lila said. "How rude!"

"But Steven said the hostess goes first," Jessica argued. "It's in all the etiquette books."

"Not the ones I've ever read," Mrs. Wakefield said.

I can't believe I fell for that! Jessica thought, glaring at her brother.

"Well, uh, sorry." Jessica set her plate down on the table and stepped out of the way. "You guys go ahead and eat. *I'll* start trimming the tree," Jessica said. "Don't pay any attention to me at all. Just enjoy your meal." She turned to Steven. "Thanks a lot!"

"I was only trying to help," he said with a smirk.

"Yeah, help embarrass me in front of everyone!" Jessica whispered fiercely. "Just stay out of my way from now on!"

She walked from the dining room table over to the corner of the living room where the tree was standing. Then she carefully lifted Elizabeth's fragile homemade glass ornament out of the box. She waited a minute, until it looked as though a few people had made it through the buffet line—most importantly, Mike. She wasn't trimming the tree just for the fun of it, after all. She was doing it so that he'd notice her.

"I think I'll put this red ornament right here, next to the green lightbulb," she said loudly, stealing Mandy's idea. "That way, the colors will reflect off each other." *Or whatever it was that made Mandy sound so artistic.*

Jessica was about to slip the hook over a branch when she turned to look at Mike, hoping that he was watching her. She managed to put the hook firmly onto a branch this time. *No mistakes,* she told herself.

But as she removed her hand from the ornament, she realized that she'd put the hook over the tiniest branch on the tree. It wasn't even a branch—it was a really long fir needle! The ornament started tumbling to the floor.

Jessica lunged to grab the glass ball. There was no way she'd break Elizabeth's favorite ornament again!

She tried to stop the ornament from falling by shoving it against the tree with her knee. But when her knee slammed into the tree, it toppled over!

"Look out!" she cried as the tree pitched toward her friends.

"Nooooo!" Lila shrieked.

Ten

Mike leaped toward Lila, grabbing the tree just before it toppled onto her head.

"Man! Close call!" Ken said, helping push the tree back up so that it was standing straight.

Just like last time, it was hardly a close call, Jessica mused. Getting hit by a Christmas tree couldn't hurt that much, could it?

Mike leaned over and adjusted the screws on the tree stand to hold it more firmly in place. "There. That should do it," he said, standing back up and brushing some needles off his palms. "Are you OK?" he asked Lila.

"I'm fine. Wow, I can't thank you enough. You're so *brave*," Lila said, gazing admiringly at Mike.

"Oh, it was nothing," Mike said modestly, shrugging. "Don't worry about it."

"No, really, Mike. It was *amazing*," Jessica added. One thing she'd learned was that Mike obviously enjoyed flattery as much as the next guy. She might as well help pile it on. "The way you leaped in front of the tree . . . you practically saved Lila's life!"

Ken rolled his eyes. "Yeah, right."

Jessica turned to him with a superior look. "You're just mad because you didn't jump to the rescue the way Mike did."

"Mike really did save me. I was so worried," Lila said breathlessly. "When I saw that trunk looming over me, about to crash onto my head . . . It was like this time I was out in the woods once, way up in Oregon, on a business trip with my father. They were cutting down gigantic trees, and this huge tree fell—right next to me!" Lila said. "I was nearly crushed!"

OK, this is a bit much, Jessica thought. "Come on, Lila. That tree—" Jessica stopped herself, remembering Mike's story about his great-grandfather. She wouldn't stick her foot in her mouth again. "That tree, Lila . . . every time I think about it, I get so upset, because it could have killed you."

"Exactly!" Lila cried. "And I just had one of those . . . what do you call them . . . ?"

"Flashbacks?" Jessica offered.

"Yes! Right here in your living room!" Lila chewed her thumbnail. "Mike, you wouldn't have believed it."

Or at least you shouldn't, Jessica thought. *Because I've heard the story a hundred times, and I don't believe it!* But she wanted to seem sensitive, so she gently put a hand on Lila's shoulder. "Tell us about it. Maybe that'll make you feel better. Let out the fear."

"It was such a huge tree," Lila said dramatically. "And when it hit the ground, it was like the whole forest shook. Kind of a mini-earthquake. Ever since then . . . I've been afraid—"

"She's afraid of trees," Jessica said, giving Lila a supportive hug. "Which makes sense because, as we all know, people are hurt by trees every day."

"Actually, that's not true," Mike broke in.

Huh? Jessica nearly keeled over. But he was the one who'd said that!

"Not every day. More like in freak accidents," Mike went on. "My great-grandfather was killed by a tree."

"No way!" Ken exclaimed.

Mike nodded. "A tree was struck by lightning. It cracked in half and fell over, and crashed into my great-grandfather's house, which collapsed on him. He was buried in rubble."

"Oh, Mike, I am *so* sorry," Jessica said, stepping toward Mike.

"So I know exactly how you feel," he said, taking Lila's hand and guiding her toward the couch. "Just sit down and relax."

Jessica stared at her best friend. Lila was practically

holding hands with *her* guy! She'd avoided saying something rude in front of Mike, but it hadn't gotten her anywhere. What was the point of all this if Lila ended up with him? She decided to put an end to their little private conversation about the dangers of trees. "Let's open the presents now!" Jessica said.

"But . . . we haven't finished eating," Elizabeth protested. "And Amy isn't here yet."

That's the point! Jessica thought. *We've got to get this whole present thing over with before she sets foot in this house!*

"I know, Elizabeth, but I just can't wait another minute," Jessica said. "The suspense is killing me. And I'm sure Amy wouldn't mind."

"Well, I guess it would be OK," Elizabeth said.

"I'm with Jessica," Winston said. "The suspense is killing me too. Or maybe it's the fact that I just ate three pieces of lasagna way too fast. Anyway, let's see what we've got!" He put his plate down on the floor and rubbed his hands together. "Show me the money!"

Jessica smiled. "Gee, thanks, Winston. Accordion lessons. Just what I always wanted. No, seriously! This way, my dad and I can play carols together, like you guys did tonight."

"Exactly what I was thinking," Winston said proudly.

I know! Jessica thought.

Elizabeth picked up a box and read off, "For Ellen, From Mike."

Some things you wanted to change . . . but couldn't, Jessica thought sadly as Ellen tore open the package and pulled out a purple baseball cap.

"The Utah Unicorns! Awesome! How did you know I liked basketball?" She grinned at Mike.

"And now for the final Secret Santa gift," Elizabeth said a little while later. "And I think I saved the best for last—or at least the heaviest. No offense to anyone."

"Oh, fine, Elizabeth. *Knock* my accordion lessons," Winston said, pretending to be highly insulted. "See if they let you into the Polka Hall of Fame now."

"Like you'll get in," Aaron teased him.

"Hey, for the three-fifty admission fee, anything's possible," Winston replied with a chuckle.

Did Winston have to make the same lame joke? Jessica wondered as she fidgeted with a loose piece of carpet pile.

"This is for Lila," Elizabeth said, handing her present to Mandy, who passed it to Ellen, who gave it to Lila.

"I was starting to think I wasn't going to get anything," Lila said.

"Hey, wait a second. Is that all the presents there are?" Mike asked.

"Why, did you want another?" Ken teased him.

"No, not for *me.* Elizabeth didn't get one." Mike pointed to the empty space in front of Elizabeth. "Is somebody sick?"

"No, everybody's here," Mandy said. "Except for Amy, who should be here any second. And that gift on the coffee table is for her."

"She already gave me my present," Aaron said. "She left the present with Elizabeth, remember?"

"Well then . . . who was supposed to get Elizabeth a gift?" Mike asked.

"So, Lila, open your present," Jessica urged.

Lila tore off the wrapping paper and pulled out the photo album. "Lila's Yearbook," she read out loud. "Cool!" She flipped through the first few pages, admiring the photographs and laughing at the captions. "This is so awesome!"

She showed the album to Janet and Mandy, who were sitting beside her. "Look at all these pictures of me—and us. It's so thoughtful. Who made this? It must have taken hours! Who gave this to me?" Lila asked.

"Read the tag!" Elizabeth said excitedly.

Jessica smiled. Everything was going exactly according to plan. "Yeah, Lila, find the tag."

Lila rustled through the crumpled ball of wrapping paper. "To Lila, From Jessica," she read out loud. "I should have known! Only Jessica knows me this well." She beamed a smile across the circle at Jessica. "Wow, how did you ever come up with such a great idea?"

"J-Jessica?" Elizabeth sputtered. Before Elizabeth could finish her sentence, the doorbell rang.

Jessica couldn't believe her ears. *Please tell me*

Steven ordered a pizza. Please tell me that's not Amy! She's supposed to be baking all night!

Steven was sitting by the door, and he hopped up to answer it. "Hey, Amy!" he said. "Come on in."

Amy rushed into the house, tossing her jacket onto a chair. "Oh, no! Did I miss everything?" She looked around the circle.

"Not quite," Elizabeth told her in a muted tone.

Jessica decided to try to change the subject—that was her only hope now! "What about all those gingerbread houses you're making? How's that going? Do you think you'll help raise a lot of money?"

"If I never see another gingerbread house again, it'll be too soon," Amy said with a groan. Everyone laughed. "We were only supposed to make ten, right? And then they call my mom this morning and ask if we can do ten *more*."

"Wow. That's a lot of work," Elizabeth said, raising her eyebrows.

"Exactly. They have to be ready by tomorrow, apparently. So my mom and I went into turbo mode, and we were making all these walls that weren't fitting together. So finally, she decided we could never finish them by tomorrow, and she told me to take off." Amy clapped her hands together, and powdered sugar drifted to the floor. "So, Lila," she said, pointing to the gift in Lila's hands. "What did you think of that photo album Elizabeth made for you? Isn't it incredible?"

"*Elizabeth* made this for me?" Lila asked.

"Yeah, I happened to bust in on her when she was working on it, so she had to tell me it was for you," Amy admitted. "Kind of blew the whole Secret Santa thing, but I didn't tell anyone else."

"Wait a second. Did you help Jessica with this?" Lila asked Elizabeth.

"No," Elizabeth admitted, shaking her head. "I made it all myself."

"Then why is Jessica's name on the tag?" Lila flipped the photo album to the first page. "And her name's on the inscription too. Wait a second." Lila glanced at Jessica as she peeled off the gold-foil sticker. "For Lila, Happy Christmas Memories from Elizabeth!" Lila dropped the photo album on the floor and stared at Jessica. "You stole this gift from Elizabeth! You tried to pass it off as your own!"

"I . . . no, I didn't," Jessica fumbled for words.

"So you didn't give anyone a gift, did you?" Aaron said, stunned.

"You didn't *buy* anything," Janet said.

"I can't believe you," Lila said. "Pretending to give me a present like that. Who were you supposed to buy for anyway?"

"Yeah, who didn't get to have a Secret Santa?" Mike asked. Then he clapped his hand over his mouth. "Oh my gosh. Elizabeth."

OK, I think we've reached crisis stage. Jessica didn't see much point in sticking around for the rest of the insults. She got to her feet and started slowly backing out of the room. Where had she gone wrong?

"It was a . . . a mistake!" she said. "It could have happened to anybody!"

"Yeah, anybody who doesn't have a *heart*," Ellen said.

Jessica felt a tear trickle down her cheek. "I don't care what any of you think. I hate all of you!"

She ran upstairs and slammed the door to her bedroom. Then she collapsed on her bed and burst into sobs. Why did everything keep turning out wrong? Why did her life have to be so horrible? It wasn't fair!

"I wish this day had never happened!" she gulped between sobs.

Eleven

Jessica yawned, blinking her eyes a few times as she adjusted to the bright morning sunlight streaming through her window. It had been sunny the day before, but she wasn't going to assume it was her third Christmas Eve in a row. It was sunny most days in southern California. That didn't mean anything.

A car outside on the street honked its horn. Jessica closed her eyes. From the bathroom, she heard the shower knobs squeak.

Unfortunately, *that* meant something: *Christmas Eve, Part Three* had begun.

Jessica sighed and threw off her blankets. She slowly changed into a pair of jeans and a sweater, dreading the day that stretched out ahead of her. One rerun of a TV show was fine, but two were downright boring.

She was getting really tired of this outfit, for one thing. If the day never changed, she'd never get to do her laundry!

Her parents walked by in the hallway on their way downstairs.

"Well, I don't know if we should give the kids his cards this morning or tomorrow morning."

"Bob wants them to open the cards on Christmas Eve. There's really no point in waiting until tomorrow."

Jessica slid her feet into her clogs. *Just give us the cards already*, she thought. Did Uncle Bob's Christmas check really merit such a drawn-out discussion? He could keep the money, if it meant she wouldn't have to hear the same discussion at the breakfast table that morning.

She slouched downstairs to the kitchen, where Steven and Elizabeth were already seated at the breakfast table. She didn't say, "Good morning." What was the point?

"Good morning, Jessica," Mrs. Wakefield greeted her anyway.

"Hi there." Mr. Wakefield slid into a seat opposite Steven and opened the morning newspaper to the business section.

He should have every article memorized by now, Jessica thought, staring at the toaster. Did she really want toast and cereal? Again?

Steven looked at her over the top of the sports section. "What happened to you?"

"I didn't get enough beauty sleep. I know, I know," Jessica sighed.

Steven stared at her. "Yeah. That."

Jessica rubbed her eyes. She decided not to eat anything for breakfast. Maybe if she didn't eat—if she did everything differently—she could break the vicious Christmas Eve cycle. To do that, she'd have to change the conversation too.

"So, can I ask you all a question?" she said.

"I know, I know. Can you borrow money from me for your last-minute shopping? The answer is no," Steven said.

"That's not the question. The question is, has anyone heard from Uncle Bob lately?" she asked.

"Aha!" Steven cried. "I knew that question would come up eventually."

Jessica stared at him. "You did? How did you know I was going to ask about Uncle Bob?"

"Oh. Is that what you said?" Steven looked completely stumped.

"I thought you were buying a new dress," Elizabeth said. "But I don't really need one. In fact, I think I have too many clothes."

"Yeah. Whatever, Elizabeth." Jessica rolled her eyes. Even when she cut the conversation short, Elizabeth still managed to get in something about what a good person she was, compared to her twin. "So, Mom and Dad. What about Uncle Bob?" Jessica pressed.

"No," Mr. Wakefield said abruptly.

"Not a chance," Mrs. Wakefield added.

"What do you mean? You haven't heard from him lately?" Jessica shook her head. This wasn't going to work very well if everyone else kept repeating the answers to questions that weren't even being asked anymore! She felt as if she were stuck in a parallel universe. She was speaking one language, and everyone else was speaking another!

"However, your uncle Bob might be able to help you out." Mr. Wakefield slid an envelope across the table to Jessica, then one to Elizabeth and one to Steven.

Jessica picked up the envelope. *Thank you, Uncle Bob, yet again! Wait—does this mean I have to write three thank-you notes?* She stood up and started to leave the kitchen. Everyone was so preoccupied with repeating the previous day that they didn't even notice her!

"I think we ought to bake some more cookies for the party tonight," Mrs. Wakefield announced all of a sudden. "I'm afraid we don't have nearly enough."

"Oh, OK," Elizabeth said. "That'll be fun. You're going to help, right, Jessica?"

Jessica wrinkled her nose. "Couldn't you just *buy* some more cookies with your fifty dollars?"

Oh, no! I just said the same thing I said the first Christmas Eve, Jessica realized. *I probably just blew it—again!*

She excused herself and left the table. Jessica ran

up to her room, taking the steps two at a time. She was determined to get out of this, one way or another. Logically, the only way to make the day stop repeating itself was to change *everything*. She couldn't wait to get started.

Reliving the same awful night over and over again was ruining her social life. And it was all Elizabeth's fault. Jessica almost didn't want to have the party anymore. But she still wanted to get even with Elizabeth. This time, Jessica would fix it so that there was no *way* she could get caught.

She darted into Elizabeth's room, unwrapped the photo album, and tore out the page that bore Elizabeth's inscription. Ha! She'd like to see Elizabeth find a way around that one. She wrapped it back up and changed the tag. *Now all I have to do is keep Amy from coming. . . .*

"So what did you buy?" Janet asked, pointing to Jessica's bag from Valley Fashions as she was leaving the mall that afternoon.

"A dress," Jessica said blandly.

"Let's see it!" Mandy said.

"No, I . . ." Jessica tried to remember what Ellen kept saying every time she ran into her. Something about not telling Janet what she was wearing to the party. *Hey, maybe Ellen's a lot smarter than I ever gave her credit for. If I don't show Janet the dress, she can't make fun of it. I'll get out of here faster, and I won't have to listen to those same dumb comments of hers.*

"You don't like the dress you bought?" Janet guessed. "You don't want us to see it because you just realized it's ugly? No, wait—your mom picked it out for you." She laughed.

If only I'd punched Janet in the nose the first time, I'd get to do it again and again. . . .

"No, it's not ugly," Jessica declared. "I like it a lot, in fact." *And so do you! You just don't know it yet.* "But I think we should keep our outfits secret, like the Secret Santas."

"Hey," Ellen said. "That's what *I* was thinking. Wow, that's so weird. We must have ESP or something."

"Or something," Jessica muttered under her breath.

"Aren't you even going to tell us what color it is?" Mandy asked.

"Yeah, what if we clash? What if I show up in the same dress?" Janet said. "You'd be so embarrassed."

"Oh, I'm not too worried about that," Jessica said with a confident shrug. "This was the last one they had! And they won't be getting any more until after the holidays." *Not even from returns!* Jessica thought, giving Janet a big smile.

Jessica crept up the Suttons' driveway, trying to be as quiet as a cat. *I'm sorry, Amy. But this is the only way.*

Amy was the only one who knew that Elizabeth had picked Lila's name out of the hat. She kept telling everyone how hard Elizabeth had worked on the photo album and that Jessica had stolen the gift from her sister. Well, all of that was about to end.

When I get my reputation back, Christmas will come, Jessica thought, approaching the Suttons' garage. Jessica felt certain that as soon as everything on Christmas Eve came out perfectly, Christmas would follow. She could smell all the holiday baking coming from the house, and her mouth started watering. She pictured all the delicious, elaborate gingerbread houses lined up on the kitchen counter, with powdered sugar on the roofs that looked like snow and curlicued pink icing outlining the windows and doors. . . .

Focus, Jessica! Quit drooling. You have a job to do here. You have to get in, and get out.

Jessica took a deep breath and opened the side door to the garage. There it was, the metal spokes gleaming in the sunlight streaming through the door. Amy's bike. The same bike she had ridden over to the Wakefields' house each Christmas Eve for the last two days, after helping her mother finish that last gingerbread house.

Jessica reached into her pocket and pulled out a safety pin. *Good-bye, tires. Adios, Amy. See you after Christmas!*

"Go ahead," Jessica urged. "No, go ahead. Really, please. Go ahead." She gestured toward the buffet table. "Guests first."

"Thanks!" Aaron said, plowing into the pan of lasagna and taking two giant pieces.

"Great food," Winston added, filling his plate.

"Come on, Jessica, you can go now," Steven urged her. "Miss Mannerly says—"

"Oh, no. I couldn't possibly," Jessica said. "In fact, I'll take over waiting on everyone." *I'm not letting him dupe me again with his dumb, kindly advice!*

"No way! I'm getting paid," Steven said.

"Then *do* something," Jessica urged. "*Wait* on someone. Lila, don't you need a fresh glass of mineral water?" She shoved Steven toward her and bowed to Mike, the next person in line. "Please, go right ahead. Take as much as you like."

From across the room, Jessica caught her mother beaming proudly at her. *So far, so good*, Jessica thought. She was wearing the cute red dress, and she'd sung "Jingle Bells" in a dull monotone—not too softly, not too loudly.

It looked as though this would be the night she'd finally succeed at everything.

"Jessica? Aren't you going to eat?" Elizabeth asked, pausing by the small remaining stack of plates before she picked one up.

"No, thanks. You go ahead. I think I'll start trimming the tree." Jessica gazed at the tree. Even bare, just sitting there in its stand, it looked dangerous— like it might fall at any second. And she'd already resolved never to pick up Elizabeth's favorite red glass ornament again.

"On second thought, I'll just have a seat on the couch over there," she told Elizabeth. "You guys join me to open the presents whenever you're ready." She sank into the couch, heaving a relieved sigh.

The less I do, the fewer risks I take. I am so close to getting this thing over with. Mike was going to be incredibly impressed with her gift to Lila, and everyone would think Jessica was an amazing friend. Well, except Elizabeth, of course—but she would get over it. . . . At this point, Jessica didn't really care whether or not they all loved her. She just didn't want them all to hate her!

She picked up a needle, some thread, and the bowl of cranberries and popcorn. Putting a strand of popcorn and cranberries on the tree would hardly tip it over. The good thing about old-fashioned ideas was that they weren't dangerous.

She held the threaded needle in one hand and a cranberry in the other. She tried to pierce the cranberry, but it popped out of her hand, and she jabbed the needle into her index finger instead. "Ouch! Ouch, ouch, ouch!" she cried.

She expected Mike to come to the rescue, but everyone was so busy eating and talking, they hadn't even noticed!

Maybe it's for the best, Jessica thought, putting her finger in her mouth. *I'll just sit here and wait until the cut stops bleeding. Don't mind me!*

*   *   *

"Come on, Jessica. Help me put the star on top," Lila pleaded.

"Oh, no. Thanks, Lila, but you do it," Jessica insisted. Her finger was still a little sore, and besides, she didn't want to knock the tree down yet again.

"But it brings good luck," Lila said. "And it's your tree, and your house—"

"Lila, I insist. You put the star on top," Jessica said, handing Lila the silver star. "Here. I'll get a chair for you."

As she pulled a chair over near the Christmas tree, Jessica tried not to laugh. This was going to be more perfect than she'd even imagined. This time, *Lila* would tip the tree over. And *Jessica* would be standing where Lila usually did. Mike would have to catch the tree to keep it from clobbering Jessica! Then she could give him some sob story about how she'd hated trees ever since she got a horrible splinter in her thumb when she was eight, and he could console *her*.

"Go ahead, Lila. Climb up," Jessica instructed.

Lila got onto the chair, holding the star in one hand. She leaned forward, preparing to slip it over the treetop.

Jessica scurried over next to Mike. *Here we go*, she thought excitedly. *I'm about to rewrite history.* She struck a pathetic pose and closed her eyes, trying to look helpless. Mike would have to save her now.

"There we go! All done!" Lila exclaimed.

Jessica opened her eyes and saw Lila climbing down from the chair. She stared at the tree. The star was perched on top as naturally as if it were a bird that had just landed there. "How did you do that?" she muttered.

"Lila, you're very coordinated," Mike observed.

Jessica wanted to change the ways things happened, but she was supposed to come out ahead, not behind! Well, this tree thing wasn't over yet. She could still make it tip over.

She casually walked around the tree, pretending to check out the decorations. She pushed on a few branches, but the tree didn't move. She shoved it with her knee. Nothing happened.

She moved around to the other side. She would get this thing onto the ground somehow, without anyone noticing—and she would be the one underneath it when it fell.

If I just slam the trunk with my hip here, then it will fall there, and—

Dingdong.

"Amy!" Elizabeth cried as the door swung open. "You made it!"

Twelve

◇

What? Jessica nearly cried out loud. *What about her slashed tires? She's here even earlier than the last two times. This isn't how it was supposed to work at all!*

"I thought you'd never get here!" Elizabeth exclaimed happily to Amy as she walked through the front door.

And I was hoping *you'd never get here,* Jessica thought, frowning at Amy. *Not just hoping—actively planning! So what went wrong?*

Elizabeth pushed her way past Jessica to greet Amy in person. Jessica tried to move out of the way, but she got pushed right into the Christmas tree—which promptly tipped over, right toward Lila.

"*Nooooo!*" Lila shrieked.

Jessica was starting to feel immune to Lila's

cries. *It's kind of like the little boy who cried wolf,* Jessica thought, *only it's the little girl who cried "Tree!"* Jessica wished Mike felt the same way. But, sure enough, he leaped to the rescue, and they started talking about trees—again.

I guess I should admire his consistency, Jessica thought. Night after night, he put his life on the line for Lila. But who cared? It didn't count when it wasn't Jessica's life he was saving. Or when all he was doing was saving Lila the trouble of pulling a bunch of fir needles out of her hair.

"What, uh . . . what took you so long?" Jessica asked when Amy came over to the group.

"It was *so* weird. But both my bicycle tires were flat," Amy said. "I have no idea how that happened. I mean, I can't remember riding over anything sharp, and they can't both have worn out at the same time." She shook her head, a puzzled expression on her face.

"Hmmm. How strange." Jessica shrugged. "How *bizarre.*"

"Clearly, I couldn't ride my bike. So I asked my mom to drive me over," Amy told her. "Anyway, I'm finally here. Did you start opening the presents yet?"

"N-No," Jessica stammered. "Not quite yet."

"Then let's get to it!" Amy said. "I can't wait to see who my Secret Santa is."

Jessica felt a familiar quiver in her stomach.

"I'll hand out the presents," Elizabeth offered,

scooting onto her knees as she crouched under the Christmas tree. "OK, first . . . let's start with this one." She picked up a square-shaped box.

Uh-oh, Jessica thought. *Why is she starting with that one? What happened to my perfect plan? I've got to get out of here!*

Elizabeth pretended to shake the box. "Wow, this is heavy. I wonder what it is." She grinned, then lifted the top flap of the tag to read it. Her expression turned from a smile to a frown. "Oh. This is for Lila. And it's from . . . Jessica?" she said, sounding confused.

"Wait a second. I thought you were Lila's Secret Santa," Amy said.

"I was," Elizabeth admitted.

"And *you* made that gift for Lila," Amy said. "I caught you yesterday, working on it! Right?"

"Right," Elizabeth said.

"So how come Jessica's name is on the tag?" Amy asked.

"You're sure this is from Elizabeth . . . not Jessica?" Lila asked Amy.

"I walked into her room yesterday, by mistake. Lila, that gift's from Elizabeth, not Jessica," Amy explained.

Lila turned to Jessica. "Then how come *you* signed your name to it?"

"Yeah," twenty voices said at once. "How come you signed your name?"

Jessica clapped her hands over her ears and ran

out of the room. She didn't want to hear all their accusations: "How could you do that?" and "You didn't get Elizabeth a gift?" and "You stole Elizabeth's gift and tried to take the credit?" She knew what they were going to say before they even opened their mouths.

She took her hands off her ears to open the door to her bedroom just in time to hear Lila shriek up the stairwell, "You're a rotten person, Jessica Wakefield!"

Jessica climbed into bed with all her clothes on and covered her head with the pillow so nobody would hear her sobs.

Wasn't there any way out of this nightmare?

Jessica stretched her arms over her head and rolled over in bed, staring up at the ceiling. She heard a car honking outside. Jessica covered her ears. *No! Not again!*

Elizabeth, I never thought I'd say this, but please don't take a shower today. Stringy, greasy hair is OK— you can get away with it by saying it's the grunge look. It's just for one day. Tomorrow you can start bathing again and—

Squeak!

"No," Jessica muttered, rolling back and forth in her bed. "No!" She felt like she was on a really awful ride in an amusement park, and it wouldn't stop.

"Well, I don't know if we should give the kids

his cards this morning or tomorrow morning," her mother said as she passed by Jessica's door.

Jessica groaned. *Don't give us any cards—from Uncle Bob or anyone else. Ever again!*

"Bob wants them to open the cards on Christmas Eve. There's really no point in waiting until tomorrow," her father replied.

No, it can't be, Jessica thought desperately as she staggered out of bed and looked at her haggard reflection in the mirror. But it was. The fourth Christmas Eve in a row. And she looked as awful as she felt.

What did she do when she couldn't face something—or someone—at school? Simple. She stayed in bed. Jessica crawled back under the covers, pressing her cheek into her pillow.

What was the point of going down to breakfast anyway? She knew what everyone was going to say. It hadn't even been that interesting the first time!

"Jessica? What are you still doing in bed?" Mrs. Wakefield walked into Jessica's bedroom and sat on the edge of the bed. "We have lots to do today."

"I don't feel so hot," Jessica said. She faked a cough.

"There wasn't anything wrong with you yesterday," her mother commented, placing her hand on Jessica's forehead.

Who could remember yesterday? Jessica thought.

She'd had three identical days in a row. And none of them had been December 23!

"You don't feel warm. I don't think you have a fever," Mrs. Wakefield said.

"But I'm cold," Jessica lied. "And then I'm hot, then I'm cold—"

"Maybe it's because you keep throwing your blankets onto the floor." Mrs. Wakefield picked up Jessica's comforter and spread it out on the bed. "Jessica, you're not playing games with me, are you?"

"G-Games?" Jessica asked.

"Yes. It's pretty obvious to me what's going on," Mrs. Wakefield said.

"It is? Oh, Mom, you don't know how glad I am to hear that!" Jessica said, heaving a sigh of relief. "I thought I was the only one."

"The only one pretending to be sick so she can get out of helping with the party? Yes, yes, you are," Mrs. Wakefield said sternly. "And I don't appreciate it one bit!"

"No, Mom—that's not what I'm doing," Jessica said. "See, I'm staying in bed because I know what's going to happen today—"

"What's going to happen today is a lot of hard work. And we all know how you feel about hard work." Mrs. Wakefield stood up and brushed her hands together. "Well, Jessica, if you don't feel well enough to help us get ready for the party, then you can't attend the party either."

"Fine!" Jessica said. "I don't want to have the party anyway!"

"Yes, you do," Mrs. Wakefield told her. "You badgered us for weeks until we gave in."

"I changed my mind," Jessica said. "I hate parties."

"Hmmm." Mrs. Wakefield paused, her hand on the door. "Maybe you *are* sick. You'd better stay in here all day."

"Gladly," Jessica muttered, pulling the covers over her head. She wasn't getting up until Christmas!

"With a corncob pipe and a button nose and two eyes made out of coal!"

Jessica chewed on the end of her pencil. She was trying to make a list of "Ways to Make Christmas Come." But there was so much noise traveling up to her room from the party downstairs, she couldn't concentrate.

All she had so far on her list were a few phrases:

1. Don't sing.
2. Don't get in food line first.
3. Don't trim tree (two-for-one: no broken ornament, no tree tipping over).
4. Don't let Amy in the door.

Hmmm. That doesn't sound like much of a party. But it just might work. . . .

"He was made of snow but the children know . . ."

Janet's and Mike's voices rose above the din, blending in perfect harmony. Tonight, without Jessica there, the guests had decided to sing a few extra carols.

Jessica threw down her pad and pencil and turned over, pulling the covers over her head. If only she could go downstairs and sing with Mike. But she couldn't.

She felt like she'd been laying in bed for days when she finally heard the doorbell ring. That must be Amy. Not that it mattered this time, because Jessica had never gotten out of bed, had never stolen Elizabeth's gift for Lila. . . . Amy couldn't catch her in the act this time, because Jessica hadn't done anything. At least there was some satisfaction there.

A minute passed, and Jessica was just beginning to feel sleepy when she head a loud shriek.

"She didn't!"

"She couldn't!"

"What a creep!"

Wait a second. I didn't get out of bed today, except to get a glass of water. I never went into Elizabeth's room. I never went downstairs. I didn't change the tag! I didn't change the inscription! So how did I end up stealing Elizabeth's gift?

Jessica was trying to figure it all out when Steven barged into her room.

"Well, Jessica, if I were you, I'd stay in bed for the rest of my life."

I was planning on it, Jessica thought. "Really? Why?" she asked.

"As if you don't know. I still can't believe what you've done. I mean, I would never have said you were capable of something *this* devious," Steven began. "But since Elizabeth was the only one downstairs who didn't get a present, and you're the only one who wasn't at the party, it's obvious that you tried to squirm out of your Secret Santa obligation by pretending to be sick. Which is totally lame. I hope saving that whopping ten dollars was worth it," Steven said, sounding disgusted with her.

"So everyone's really mad? Even though I'm upstairs sick and not getting in their way or insulting them or knocking over the tree or anything?"

"Like you have to ask! Like you didn't know that you were planning this when you woke up this morning. Well, Jessica, you didn't get away with it this time." Steven laughed and went back downstairs.

Jessica slammed the door closed behind him. No matter what she did, whether she stayed in bed or not, she was stuck in a nightmare! And she was running out of possible solutions to her problem.

Thirteen

Jessica opened her eyes.

Go ahead. Honk. The car horn sounded. She counted off the seconds in her head. *One, two, three, now Elizabeth will turn off the squeaky shower.*

Squeak! This was turning into a drill.

Jessica tossed off the covers and climbed out of bed. As she changed out of her pajamas, her parents walked by in the hallway.

"Well, I don't know if we should give the kids his cards this morning or tomorrow morning," her mother was saying.

Jessica felt like throwing open the door and yelling, "You gave us the cards, Mom! Four times already! And the poem on the card is so corny, if I have to read it again I'll throw up!"

"Bob wants them to open the cards on Christmas

Eve. There's really no point in waiting until tomorrow," her father replied.

Technically, this is the fifth Christmas Eve in a row, Jessica thought. *Which ought to make it December 28!* If things kept up like this, Jessica was going to miss New Year's Eve. Come to think of it, if it went on long enough, she'd miss the Fourth of July. So how could she stop this never-ending repetition of the same day?

Obviously, I'm doing something wrong. And I'm going to have to live through this day again and again until I get it right.

What was that saying her social studies teacher was always repeating? Those who didn't learn from past mistakes would end up repeating them over and over again until they died. Or something like that.

The way Jessica saw it, learning from the past wasn't her problem—Amy Sutton was her problem. That was nothing new. Ever since Amy had become Elizabeth's best friend, she'd been a problem. But now it was much more serious than ever before. Now Amy was ruining her life!

Jessica had fixed everything else. She bought the right dress. She didn't sing too loudly. She didn't tip over the tree. She saved the precious ornament. She switched the tag *and* the inscription on the present for Lila. Elizabeth would never tell. But Amy would! And she kept *on* telling. Every single night!

Amy was the reason Jessica couldn't keep the fact that she stole Elizabeth's gift for Lila a secret. Amy was the one who'd caught Elizabeth making the gift in the first place. She was the only one who knew that Elizabeth was Lila's Secret Santa, not Jessica. The solution was obvious: Keep Amy from coming to the party and blowing Jessica's cover.

I have to get Amy out of the way, for real this time. But how? It wouldn't be easy to keep Elizabeth's best friend in the entire world away on Christmas Eve.

Jessica paused for a moment on the stairs, a little scared by herself. She was starting to sound like someone in a gangster movie. *Get rid of Amy? Get her out of the way?* She didn't want any actual *harm* to come to Amy. Of course, if she happened to come down with a twenty-four-hour bug, that would be *convenient*, but Jessica would never poison Amy's food or anything. There had to be an easier way. . . .

Jessica couldn't back down now. This revenge scheme had to work!

Jessica stood at the ticket window inside the Sweet Valley Civic Center. "Thanks," she said as the woman slid two tickets toward her.

"Have a wonderful time at the show tonight!"

"Oh, these aren't for me—they're for a friend," Jessica told her.

"I'm sure she'll love it. What a nice gift." The woman smiled.

Jessica didn't really care whether Amy actually liked the special Christmas Eve performance of the *Christmas on Ice* show. The important thing was getting her there. She knew that Amy had recently started taking figure skating lessons and that she was wild about them. How could she pass up an opportunity like this to see professional skaters in action?

She walked over to the pay phone in the center's lobby and dialed Amy's phone number. "Hello, is this Miss Amy Sutton?" she asked, adding a phony Russian accent to her voice.

"Yes . . . ," Amy said slowly. "Who is this?"

"This is Ludmila. Congratulations! You've won two tickets for the performance of tonight," Jessica said, trying to sound as foreign as possible.

"Performance?" Amy asked.

"Of *Christmas on Ice*. Featuring skaters from all around the world! All you have to do is pick up the tickets at the will-call window, and—"

"Wait a second. How did I win tickets?" Amy asked. "I didn't even enter a contest."

"Ah. Aha!" Jessica cried. "Yes, Ludmila realizes this is a surprise." *Too bad Jessica didn't realize you would ask this question!* Jessica thought frantically. "But you see, Miss Sutton, ah . . . aha!" Jessica had a sudden brainstorm. "Pardon me, I sneeze. I was starting to say that anyone who is taking lessons at the Sweet Valley rink was automatically entered into the contest."

"Oh. Well, in that case, cool!" Amy exclaimed. "What night did you say it was?"

"Tonight. Tonight only. Very special Christmas Eve—"

"But I can't make it tonight. I have a party to go to," Amy protested.

"Miss Sutton, I do not want to sound . . . how you say? . . . rude, but this is a chance of a lifetime," Jessica said. "These skaters will not be back in Sweet Valley. Ever!"

"Oh. Well, maybe I could change my plans. . . ."

"No maybe. You must change them!" Jessica ordered her in her deepest, sternest Russian-sounding voice.

"OK. I will," Amy said. "Thank you so much . . ."

"Ludmila. Stop at the will-call window. Do not forget!" Jessica hung up the phone and walked back to the ticket office window. "Could you please hold these here, under the name Sutton? Thanks."

"Elizabeth, you should put this one on the tree." Jessica pointed to the fragile homemade ornament.

"Are you sure you don't want to put it on?" Elizabeth asked.

"Oh, I'm sure," Jessica said. She was off to a good start tonight, and she didn't intend to blow it. She'd helped her parents prepare the snacks. She'd helped Steven take coats. She'd taken care of the candy herself, so Steven couldn't pull a practical joke on her guests. She'd complimented Janet on her green jumper and white turtleneck. She'd strung cranberries until her fingernails were dyed red. And when Lila started talking with Mike, Jessica hadn't dumped the tree onto her head.

I deserve a gold star for the way I've been acting, Jessica thought. *I hope everyone's noticing what a gracious hostess I'm being, because it isn't easy!*

"Here you go, Elizabeth." Jessica held the ornament out to her twin.

Just then, the doorbell rang. Jessica dropped the ornament, and it crashed to the floor, breaking into a hundred tiny pieces. "Oh, no! Amy!"

Elizabeth stared at her. "How do you know it's Amy? And why do you sound more upset about her coming than you do about breaking my most treasured ornament in the world?"

"I was surprised by the doorbell, that's all," Jessica said. *In fact, I think I almost had a heart attack!* "I'm so sorry about your ornament!" She crouched down and started picking up the tiny pieces.

Amy sauntered into the living room. "Hi, Elizabeth."

"Wow, you're here earlier than you thought," Elizabeth observed. "How did you manage that?"

"The weirdest thing happened." Amy took off her coat. "I won tickets to that *Christmas on Ice* show . . . for tonight."

So why aren't you there now—instead of here? Jessica stared up at Amy as she and Steven used a dustpan to sweep up the shards of glass.

"I gave the tickets to my mom, since she's an even bigger skating fan than I am, and she asked a friend to go," Amy explained. "So we finished our baking early, and she dropped me off on her way to the Civic Center."

"Awesome!" Elizabeth slapped Amy's palm, giving her a high five. "I'm so glad you're here."

That makes one of us, Jessica thought bitterly.

"Me too. So, are we going to open our presents now, or what?" Amy asked.

"We were just waiting for *you,*" Mandy told her. "Now that you're here, let's get started!"

"You guys go ahead. I—I don't feel so good all of a sudden. I think I'll go upstairs and lie down," Jessica said. She ran out of the living room and up the stairs before anyone could ask about her symptoms.

My number-one symptom? Dread! Followed by fear! In a few more minutes, everyone would realize all over again that she was a complete and utter fraud of a friend—and sister. She couldn't bear to live through it again!

"Go away, Steven! I don't want to hear it!" Jessica cried when there was a knock at her door a few minutes later. She couldn't bear any more gloating from her big brother. Hadn't he said enough the night before? *Or was it the night before the night before?* Jessica wondered. She couldn't keep any of the days straight anymore. In any case, didn't he know when enough was enough?

"It's not Steven. It's me."

Jessica bolted upright on her bed. "Elizabeth?"

"Can I come in?" Elizabeth asked.

Jessica resisted the urge to say no. "I guess," she said, reaching over to unlock her door.

"Jessica, are you feeling all right?" Elizabeth sat on the edge of the bed and put her hand on Jessica's arm. "I was so worried when you ran upstairs."

"Oh!" Jessica said. "Sure—I'm fine."

"But you said you felt sick. And it's not like you to leave a party early even if you *do* feel bad," Elizabeth commented.

"No," Jessica admitted. "It isn't." *At least, not until lately.*

"So what's wrong?" Elizabeth asked. "Did somebody say something to you? You know, that upset you?"

"No." Jessica shook her head. "I'm OK. I just . . . kind of got a stomachache, that's all. I think I should stay up here for a little while."

"A stomachache? Did you eat too much?" Elizabeth asked.

"I might have," Jessica said. At the moment, Elizabeth was being so nice to her that she was starting to *get* a stomachache. She felt rotten. "But don't worry about me. Go back downstairs to the party!" she urged her sister.

"I can't go back down there, when you're up here," Elizabeth said.

"You can't?" Jessica asked. "Yes, you can. You don't want to sit around with boring old me and my aching tummy, when you could be opening presents and laughing and—"

"Jessica, it's *our* party. It's no fun without you," Elizabeth said. "Don't you realize that we've *never* spent Christmas Eve apart?"

"We . . . we haven't?" Jessica asked.

"No. And I'm not about to start now. The party can go on without me—at least for a little while," Elizabeth said. "Janet was starting to bug me anyway." Elizabeth sat down next to Jessica. "I can't think of anybody I'd rather be with right now than you."

Now Jessica's stomach started to hurt in earnest. She felt like such a heel! Here was Elizabeth, unable to enjoy the party without *her* presence. . . . And Jessica deliberately hadn't bought Elizabeth a gift. And she had stolen Elizabeth's gift for Lila— not just once, but many times in a row. Jessica didn't deserve Elizabeth. And it was time to tell her just what a creep she had for a sister.

"Elizabeth, there's something I have to tell you," Jessica began. "It's about the Secret Santa thing. I forgot—no, I didn't forget. I mean, at first I did, but then I more, like, overlooked it. The gift, I mean. I didn't get anything. So then I tried to make up for it, but that turned out all wrong too. In fact, I owe you a huge apology because—"

"Jessica!" Lila suddenly burst into the room. "Oh my gosh. Thank you so much for the excellent personal yearbook and photo album! You're so thoughtful! You're such a great friend!"

Jessica squirmed uncomfortably on the bed. "M-Me?"

Elizabeth looked at Jessica, her mouth hanging open. Suddenly, her eyes filled with tears.

I really hurt her feelings, Jessica realized. *Elizabeth feels terrible right now.* Jessica had thought that getting revenge on her sister would feel wonderful, but instead, seeing Elizabeth so upset made Jessica feel terrible too. She felt worse than she ever had before—as if she'd deliberately set out to break Elizabeth's heart. Which she sort of had.

"So, Jessica, how did you get the idea for this?" Lila turned to Elizabeth. "Look at this. Isn't it amazing?" she asked.

Why doesn't she know yet? Jessica wondered. Amy must have been out of the room when Lila opened her gift. Or else she decided not to say anything. So here was Jessica's big chance to get away with her lie!

But all of a sudden, she didn't want to get away with anything anymore. *Why did I ever want to get back at Elizabeth anyway?* Jessica wondered. She wanted Lila to know that Elizabeth was the thoughtful one. Jessica was the one who cared more about how she looked than how her friends—how her very own twin sister—felt.

"Lila, that wasn't from—" Jessica began.

"It wasn't that hard for her, actually," Elizabeth interrupted her, standing up. "Jessica knows you so well. She got the idea almost immediately."

Jessica stared at her twin. Why was she covering for her? Didn't she want the credit for creating such a great present?

"She put a lot of hard work into that album," Elizabeth continued. "She hardly did anything else for a whole day."

Stop! Jessica almost yelled. *That wasn't me, that was you! And you're going to make me cry!* In fact, Jessica was so upset that she couldn't say anything at all.

"You're the best," Lila said. She reached over and hugged Jessica. "Come back downstairs when you feel better!" She ran off, and Jessica took a deep breath.

"Elizabeth, I'm so sorry. I know you hate me right now, and you should," she began.

"But I don't," Elizabeth protested, shaking her head. Any signs that she had been tearful, or on the verge of crying, were gone. "I don't hate you at all. You're my sister. And my best friend."

"But I stole your present! I wanted Lila to think I made it," Jessica argued. "And I couldn't even manage to buy you a lousy pair of earrings!"

Elizabeth shrugged. "I don't need earrings. And any time I put into making that album, it was worth it, just seeing her reaction right now."

"Wait. Wait a second. Elizabeth, yell at me! Scream at me! Something," Jessica pleaded. "I'm totally in the wrong here. You can't let me just take your gifts and give them away as if they were my own. That's not fair."

"Maybe it isn't fair, but what's the difference,

really? I don't think I could make you feel worse than you already do, so what's the point?" Elizabeth asked. "Giving is always more fun than receiving anyway. And by letting you take credit for Lila's gift, it's almost like I'm giving two gifts at once."

"And it's almost like I'm giving *negative* two," Jessica pointed out. "How can you not be mad at me?"

"Jessica, it's Christmas Eve. I couldn't hate anybody tonight, least of all you." Elizabeth hugged her quickly. "Merry Christmas! I'll see you downstairs, when you're ready."

Elizabeth closed the door quietly behind her. Jessica sat on her bed thinking for a long time. Finally, she walked over to the window. She watched as Ken, Aaron, and Winston ran out to the Egberts' waiting minivan. They were laughing and shoving each other around, tossing their presents back and forth as if they were footballs.

They really had a good time tonight, Jessica thought. *And so did everyone else. And I should have too. Everything went the way I wanted.*

Jessica burst into tears and flopped down on her bed. *No!* she suddenly realized. *Nothing went the way I wanted! I was phony, and selfish, and I lied, on top of everything else.*

And now she'd never get another Christmas Eve to make it right, because this Christmas Eve was the final one. She knew it was, because she had finally gotten away with everything. Too bad she felt awful about it.

Fourteen

The minute Jessica opened her eyes, she shut them again. *I don't want to get up,* she thought. *I don't want to open any presents. I don't deserve them. I don't deserve to ever receive another present again in my entire life!*

Honk.

Jessica opened one eye. *What's that?* she wondered.

Squeak.

Could it be? Was she that lucky? But no, she couldn't possibly get another chance—not after all the chances she'd blown. This must be a coincidence.

Just as she turned over in bed, about to bury her head underneath the pillow, she heard her parents walk by in the hallway, on their way downstairs.

"Well, I don't know if we should give the kids his cards this morning or tomorrow morning."

"Bob wants them to open the cards on Christmas Eve. There's really no point in waiting until tomorrow," her father replied.

Yes! Jessica sat up, and a huge grin spread across her face. It *was* another chance at Christmas Eve! She leaped out of bed and quickly changed from her flannel pajamas into a pair of jeans and a sweater. She had a lot to do that day. She had to get moving.

Jessica slid her feet into her brown suede clogs, opened her door, and walked downstairs to the kitchen. On the way, she paused outside Elizabeth's room. She could see the photo album all wrapped, sitting on her desk.

She smiled and kept walking. She wasn't going to tamper with Elizabeth's present today. Not for anything in the world.

Steven and Elizabeth were sitting at the kitchen table. "Good morning, everyone," Jessica said cheerfully.

"Good morning, Jessica," Mrs. Wakefield greeted her.

"Hi there." Mr. Wakefield slid into a seat opposite Steven and opened the morning newspaper to the business section.

Steven looked at her over the top of the sports section. "What happened to you?"

"What do you mean?" Jessica asked.

"I think you should go back to bed," Steven said. "You could use a few more hours' worth of beauty sleep."

"Yeah, you're probably right," Jessica replied, rubbing her eyes. "I am tired."

Steven stared at her. "I was trying to insult you, and you didn't even notice? You must be tired."

"Hey, what did I tell you? Anyway, Steven, I'm glad you're here," Jessica said. "I need to ask you a question."

"I know, I know. Can you borrow money from me for your last-minute shopping? The answer is no," Steven said.

"That's not the question." Jessica took a sip of orange juice. "Do you know someone at school named Miranda McClusky?"

Steven shook his head. "No."

"Oh. Well, maybe you should meet her. Her brother's in our class, and he's really nice," Jessica said.

"That's it?" Steven said. "You don't want me to tell her that you like him or something dumb like that?"

"No. They're new in town." Jessica shrugged. "Just trying to be friendly and make them feel welcome."

"Oh." Steven looked confused. "Well, that's kind of nice. I'll keep my eye out for her, OK?"

"Thanks. So, is everyone looking forward to

tonight's party?" she asked, snapping open a napkin and putting it in her lap.

"Not exactly," Steven said. "I know you guys are
paying me, but I feel like I'm going to be run
ragged."

"Oh. Well, you don't have to help that much,"
Jessica said. "I mean, if we all pitch in . . ."

Steven looked across the table at Jessica. "Are
you really going to pitch in?"

Jessica nodded. "Of course!"

"Yeah, right," Steven mumbled to Elizabeth.
"I'll believe it when I see it. Next year *I'm* throwing a holiday party—and *you* guys will have to
help."

"No problem," Elizabeth told him, smiling.

"That'll be fun," Jessica said. "We'll owe you."

"Huh?" Steven shook his head and started reading the newspaper again.

"So, Jessica. What are you wearing tonight?"
Elizabeth asked.

"Oh, I don't know," Jessica said. "I figure between your closet and my closet, we'll come up
with something."

"You're not buying a new dress?" Elizabeth
sounded shocked.

"I don't think so. I've got other shopping
that's more important to do," Jessica told her.
"The party favors, for one. I want to pick out the
best candy I can find." She glanced at her father
and smiled. "*Within* the budget. And then there's

the Secret Santa gift I still need to pick out."

"Oh, I see. Well, uh, I don't know if you'd be interested in this at all—don't feel pressured," Elizabeth said. "But last night, I was building up a huge collection of clothes I don't wear or that don't fit anymore, to give away to charity. Do you have some to add?"

"Definitely," Jessica said. "I've got some stuff that wasn't even trendy two years ago."

"Well, great. Sweet Valley Home Services is having a special clothing drive, because of the holidays," Elizabeth said. "So if you come across anything . . ."

"I'll add it to the pile," Jessica said.

"Well, since you're both in the spirit of giving this morning, maybe I should join in. Here, these came from your uncle Bob." Mr. Wakefield slid an envelope across the table to Jessica, and then gave one each to Elizabeth and Steven.

Jessica opened the envelope. "Season's Greetings to My Niece," the card said. "For someone who's sweet, and just as neat. A gift from the heart, though we're far apart."

"Wow. What a nice card," Jessica said.

"Kind of corny, don't you think?" Steven wrinkled his nose.

"Yeah, but he misses us," Jessica said. "He's allowed to be corny."

"Hey, he can be as corny as he wants, if he's going to send us checks!" Steven remarked, examining the check that fell out of his card onto the table.

"Steven . . ." Mr. Wakefield said in a warning tone.

"Wow! He usually only gives us ten dollars," Jessica said.

"You're complaining?" Steven scoffed.

"No, never. Anything he gives us is nice. Even this card," Jessica said.

"It's so generous. I think I'll add this to my donation to the clothing drive," Elizabeth said.

"You know what? I think I will too," Jessica said. "I can't think of anything I really need all that much." She signed the back of the check.

Mrs. Wakefield smiled. "Well, you two are certainly in the holiday spirit. I'll be happy to drive you and your stuff over there later today," Mrs. Wakefield said. "But first, I think we ought to bake some more cookies for the party tonight. I'm afraid we don't have nearly enough."

"Oh, OK," Elizabeth said. "That'll be fun. You're going to help, right, Jessica?"

"Sure. Not this morning—I have to go to the mall and get a present for my Secret Santa person. But after that, I can definitely help," Jessica said. "Oh, wait. First, I have to get the party favors ready. Then prepare the cranberries and popcorn. *Then* I'll help with the cookies."

"You know what? You have too much to do," Elizabeth said. "I'll do the cookies."

"No way!" Jessica said. "If this is an old-fashioned Christmas, and we're making old-fashioned sugar cookies, then I have to help. It's our party, remember?"

"Sure." Elizabeth smiled. "Of course I remember."

"Great. I'll meet you back here at three," Jessica promised.

"Jessica? Jessica?"

Jessica waved at Danielle, who was standing in the doorway of Valley Fashions, and kept walking. She didn't have time to try on clothes. She had to get home and help Elizabeth with the party. Now that she had picked up the perfect earrings for Elizabeth at Total Trends, she had to get out of the mall!

"Hi, Jessica! What did you buy?" Janet asked. Behind her were Mandy and Ellen.

Jessica stopped in the doorway to the mall, halfway in and halfway out. She glanced down at the bag in her hands. She half expected to see the familiar Valley Fashions logo on the outside. But it wasn't from there—it was from Total Trends.

"Oh, it's my Secret Santa gift, that's all," Jessica told them. "No big deal."

Janet looked a little disappointed. "You're not going to tell us who it's for?"

"Of course not," Jessica said. "That would ruin everything."

"Maybe it's one of us," Ellen said. "That would be cool. I bet you give the nicest gifts, Jessica."

Jessica shifted the bag in her hands, feeling

uncomfortable. Nothing could be further from the truth! "I don't know. I just hope she—or he," Jessica added hastily, "likes it."

"Yeah, well, I'm sure she—or he—will," Janet said. "But I thought you were going to buy a new dress for the party. That's what you said yesterday. So did you get one or not?"

"No, I decided not to," Jessica said. "I looked through my closet and found a couple of outfits that'll be just fine."

"Just fine?" Janet's face turned a little pale. "I thought you had a crush on Mike McClusky."

"I do," Jessica said.

"So why aren't you going all out to impress him?" Janet asked.

"That never works," Jessica said. "Believe me. *Never.* I just decided that he'll either like me or he won't." She shrugged.

"Jessica, you don't have the flu, do you?" Mandy reached up and pressed the back of her palm against Jessica's forehead. "You're not acting normal."

"Normal for you, that is," Ellen added, a puzzled expression on her face.

"I guess I've got a lot on my mind," Jessica said. "Like right now, I have to rush home so I can wrap my Secret Santa gift and then start helping with all the party preparations. You wouldn't believe how many cookies we need to bake! See you guys tonight!" Jessica headed off down the sidewalk toward the rack where she'd locked her bicycle.

Before she got onto her bike, she tucked the small bag with Elizabeth's gift into the inside pocket of her jacket. So far, so good!

"Everything ready?" Mrs. Wakefield asked.

"Ready!" Jessica declared.

"Man the battle stations," Mr. Wakefield joked.

Just then, the doorbell rang, and everyone turned to Steven. "Well?" Jessica prompted.

Then she caught herself. *Wait—what am I doing?* "I'll get it," Jessica offered. "They're my friends." She hurried over to the door and opened it wide.

"Jessica! Hi!" Lila said, striding through the door. "Daddy let us use the limo so all the Unicorns could come at once."

"Great!" Jessica said. "Hey, give me your coats."

"It's OK," Steven said, coming to the rescue just before Jessica was buried in fabric. "I'll do it." He smiled at Jessica.

"Thanks, Steven. Remember, I owe you one next year," Jessica said.

"Oh, I'm remembering. I'm making a list, right here," he said, laughing as he tapped the side of his head.

Jessica turned around and looked at Janet. She was wearing the red dress. "That dress is so cool!" Jessica told her.

"It doesn't clash with my hair?" Janet asked nervously.

"Not at all. Now, come in and have some punch," Jessica said, leading her friends toward the lavishly decorated dining room table.

After they started helping themselves to beverages, Jessica sneaked back into the living room. She'd been home all afternoon, but she'd been busy. She still had something very important to take care of. Jessica crouched under the Christmas tree, being careful not to disturb anything.

"Jessica? What are you doing?"

"Elizabeth!" Jessica stood up so suddenly, she banged her head on the branch above her. Fir needles rained down onto the presents below. "I was, uh, just, uh, putting my present under the tree," Jessica said.

"Are you *sure?*" Elizabeth asked. "I think I caught you doing something else."

"Something else? Like what?" Jessica asked slowly.

"I think you were just rustling around down there, looking for the gift with *your* name on it." Elizabeth asked, a teasing twinkle in her eye.

Jessica smiled. "No, Elizabeth. I really was putting my present under the tree. But no peeking!"

"Sorry I'm so late," Mike said, walking into the living room after they'd all sung "Jingle Bells." "My ride got kind of messed up."

"Oh, that's OK," Jessica told him. "I'm just glad you could make it."

"Refreshments are served!" Steven announced, standing in the doorway to the dining room.

"But we only got to sing one carol," Mandy complained.

"We'll sing more later. Right, Dad?" Jessica asked.

"Yes, we'll have more carols—don't worry," Mr. Wakefield assured the crowd. "You'll sing even better after you've had a bite to eat."

"Come on, Mike. Let's get you some food," Jessica said, guiding him into the dining room. Jessica picked up a plate and handed it to Mike. "Guests first!"

"Are you sure you don't want to go ahead?" Mike asked politely.

"No, thanks. To tell you the truth, I ate too much cookie dough," Jessica confessed. "I might have some salad, but I'll wait a little bit."

Mike smiled. "What kind of cookies?"

"Sugar cookies. The kind you use cookie cutters to cut into shapes and put colored sugar on?" You can tell the ones I made. They're all in the shape of Santa Claus. It's my favorite one."

"Then I'll try one," Mike said, putting a red Santa Claus on the edge of his plate. "After I have some of this lasagna!"

"Who wants to trim the tree?" Elizabeth asked, once everyone had finished eating.

"Let's do it," Mandy said, getting to her feet. "I love putting ornaments on the tree. Not to mention ribbons, popcorn chains—"

"Mandy once made a string of old library cards and strung them around the tree," Ellen told everyone. "It was so cool."

"That must have looked pretty funky," Mike commented. "Maybe I'll do that with our tree at home this year. My parents would have a cow, though." He laughed.

"Hey, did you guys see this ornament?" Jessica asked, rummaging in the box until she pulled out a delicate red glass ornament with silver and gold swirls painted on it. "Isn't it cool?"

"I've never seen an ornament like that before," Mike said. "Where did you get it?"

"Elizabeth made it when we were younger. Actually, I made one too, but . . . it didn't look anything like this. It looked like a gold blob, actually," Jessica confessed. "It broke a long time ago, thank goodness."

"Jessica, it wasn't *that* bad," Elizabeth said.

"Oh, no? Then how come I was the only one who put it on the tree every year?" Jessica asked. She walked around the tree. "So, where should I put it?"

"Right next to that green light," Mandy said. "Then the green will light up the red glass."

"Good idea," Jessica said. She carefully slipped the hook over the branch and before turning around, made sure it was securely fastened. "Well? How does it look?"

"Beautiful," Mandy said. "Who wants to put the star on top?"

"I do," Lila said.

"OK. Go ahead. I'll hold the chair for you," Jessica offered.

"Wait—let me get my camera first!" Elizabeth ran into the kitchen and came back out, carrying her camera.

Jessica pulled a chair over beside the tree, and Lila climbed up, holding the shiny metal star in her right hand. "Ready?" she asked Elizabeth.

"Yes," Elizabeth said, lifting the camera to her eye and turning on the flash.

Lila leaned toward the tree, carefully starting to slip the star over the top.

"Here we go. One, two . . . ," Elizabeth chanted.

Jessica smiled at Lila as she reached over and put the star on the treetop. "Perfect!"

"Three!" everyone sang at once.

"Next up," Elizabeth said, reaching for a small box under the tree. "This one's for Jessica. How exciting. And it's from . . . Winston Egbert!"

Winston nodded proudly. "And I hope you'll have as much fun opening it as I did wrapping it."

Jessica took off the wrapping paper and opened the box. Inside was another box. And another box. "This is a trick!" She laughed. "No fair, Winston."

Finally, Jessica pulled a gold piece of paper rolled like a scroll from the smallest box. "Excellent! A gift certificate!" she said.

"A very personal gift certificate," Winston said, sounding a bit mischievous. Jessica smiled. She knew what the gift was, of course, and seeing how amused Winston was by his own little prank made Jessica want to laugh out loud.

Jessica unrolled the paper. Inside was a green piece of construction paper, shaped like an accordion. "This entitles you to three accordion lessons at the House of Egbert Music Hall. Retail value: $10. You'll be playing polkas in no time!" Jessica smiled. "Accordion lessons. Cool! Can you teach me how to play 'Jingle Bells'?"

"All in good time. First, I think you might want to start with something basic. Like, the *scales*," Winston joked.

"Oh, sure. But I've got three lessons," Jessica reminded him. "And I'm a fast learner." She winked at him.

"Next gift!" Jessica stared as Elizabeth picked up a box and read off, "For Ellen, From Mike."

Ellen tore open the package and pulled out a purple baseball cap. "The Utah Unicorns! Awesome! How did you know I liked basketball?" She grinned at Mike.

"Oh, a little friend . . . I mean, bird . . . gave me some advice." He smiled warmly at Jessica, who smiled back.

*   *   *

"That photo album is so awesome," Lila said. "I can't thank you enough, Elizabeth!"

"You're welcome," Elizabeth said. "So, I guess that's it for the gifts." She looked around the bottom of the tree.

"Hey, wait a second. Is that really all the presents there are?" Mike asked.

"Why, did you want another?" Ken teased him.

"No, not for *me*. Elizabeth didn't get one." Mike pointed to the empty space in front of Elizabeth. "Who was supposed to get Elizabeth a gift?" he asked.

"I was," Jessica said proudly. "And here it is." She stood up and took a tiny box out from under the Christmas tree, placing it in Elizabeth's hand. "Merry Christmas!"

"To my twin, who celebrates the joy of giving three hundred and sixty-five days a year," Elizabeth read out loud.

"Wow," Amy said. "How thoughtful, Jessica."

Elizabeth opened the box and took out the silver typewriter earrings. "I love them!" she cried. "They're so cute! Thanks, Jessica."

"You're welcome," Jessica said. Elizabeth was right. It was more fun giving gifts than receiving them.

"So, uh, Jessica." Mike came over to her as she started cleaning up all the discarded wrapping paper from the floor. "What are you doing over

Christmas vacation? I think the Utah Unicorns are coming to town. Do you want to go to a basketball game together?"

"I'd love to," Jessica told him. *You have no idea how much!* "Give me a call tomorrow. No, not tomorrow," she said. Just in case Christmas finally did arrive. "Better make it the day after tomorrow."

Fifteen

◇

Jessica opened one eye and looked warily around her room, afraid to move. She heard a noise and groaned. Was that a car horn?

No. It was Steven's alarm, honking again and again until she heard him slam his palm on the snooze button.

If the car horn didn't honk . . . Jessica was just starting to feel hopeful when she heard a loud squeaking sound. *Rats! The shower!*

But it didn't sound like the shower. It kept squeaking! So what was it?

It squeaked again. Jessica felt a flash of panic at the thought that it might be mice—until she realized that it was the sound of her squeaky doorknob being turned.

"Merry Christmas!" Elizabeth cried, running into the room. She jumped on the end of Jessica's bed.

"Christmas? It's Christmas?" Jessica asked.

"Yes," Elizabeth said.

"Really?"

"Yes."

"Finally?"

"Yes! Why, what did you think it was? Easter?" Elizabeth teased. "The Fourth of July? St. Patrick's Day?"

"Well . . ." Jessica decided to spare Elizabeth the story of the six Christmas Eves she'd just gone through. It would take too long, and Elizabeth would never believe her anyway. Maybe it had all been a nightmare. Maybe that was why it kept happening, over and over, and why she kept *thinking* she was waking up to a new morning, but it was really the same day, because it was the same nightmare. . . .

Her nose twitched. What was that delicious smell wafting up the stairs? "Is . . . is that cinnamon coffee cake baking?" she asked Elizabeth.

"Of course it is," Elizabeth said. "Which means Mom and Dad are up. Which means we won't have to wait forever for them in order to open our presents."

"Presents!" Jessica yelled. "Then it's really Christmas?"

"How many times do I have to tell you? Boy, what happened to you? Did the Christmas tree hit you on the head when you were sneaking around underneath it looking for your presents last night?" Elizabeth asked. "You're out of it this morning."

"I am *so* out of it," Jessica said, a grin spreading across her face. *I'm out of that awful, horrible time-warp nightmare!* And Jessica had never been happier to see Christmas come in her entire life.

"Come on, Elizabeth. Last one downstairs has to cook Steven's eggs for breakfast!" Jessica flung her covers to the floor and leaped out of bed.

She collided with Steven in the hallway, and Elizabeth dashed ahead of her down the stairs.

"By the way? I like my eggs scrambled," Steven said.

"You know what? I'm in such a good mood right now, I'll cook you a soufflé," Jessica offered, rushing down the staircase behind Steven.

"OK, but only if you can make it in the shape of a reindeer," Steven teased her.

Jessica was about to snap at him, but then she caught herself. There was no point in being irritated by Steven today. It was Christmas, after all.

"I'll make it in the shape of Santa Claus," she offered.

"Now *this* I have to see," Steven said as the three of them bounded into the living room.

Mr. and Mrs. Wakefield were sitting next to the Christmas tree, sipping from mugs of coffee.

"What took you guys so long?" Mr. Wakefield asked. "We've been up for hours!"

"Never mind what took us so long," Jessica said, sitting down beside her father. "Let's just all be glad that Christmas is finally here!"

"I couldn't have said it better myself." Mrs. Wakefield reached over and gave Jessica a warm hug.

"Merry Christmas, Mom," Jessica said. "Now, let's open these presents before I die of suspense!"

And she meant that. No one had been waiting for Christmas longer than Jessica had!

Bantam Books in the SWEET VALLEY TWINS series.
Ask your bookseller for the books you have missed.

#1	BEST FRIENDS	#24	JUMPING TO CONCLUSIONS
#2	TEACHER'S PET	#25	STANDING OUT
#3	THE HAUNTED HOUSE	#26	TAKING CHARGE
#4	CHOOSING SIDES	#27	TEAMWORK
#5	SNEAKING OUT	#28	APRIL FOOL!
#6	THE NEW GIRL	#29	JESSICA AND THE BRAT ATTACK
#7	THREE'S A CROWD	#30	PRINCESS ELIZABETH
#8	FIRST PLACE	#31	JESSICA'S BAD IDEA
#9	AGAINST THE RULES	#32	JESSICA ONSTAGE
#10	ONE OF THE GANG	#33	ELIZABETH'S NEW HERO
#11	BURIED TREASURE	#34	JESSICA, THE ROCK STAR
#12	KEEPING SECRETS	#35	AMY'S PEN PAL
#13	STRETCHING THE TRUTH	#36	MARY IS MISSING
#14	TUG OF WAR	#37	THE WAR BETWEEN THE TWINS
#15	THE OLDER BOY	#38	LOIS STRIKES BACK
#16	SECOND BEST	#39	JESSICA AND THE MONEY MIX-UP
#17	BOYS AGAINST GIRLS	#40	DANNY MEANS TROUBLE
#18	CENTER OF ATTENTION	#41	THE TWINS GET CAUGHT
#19	THE BULLY	#42	JESSICA'S SECRET
#20	PLAYING HOOKY	#43	ELIZABETH'S FIRST KISS
#21	LEFT BEHIND	#44	AMY MOVES IN
#22	OUT OF PLACE	#45	LUCY TAKES THE REINS
#23	CLAIM TO FAME	#46	MADEMOISELLE JESSICA

Sweet Valley Twins Super Editions

#1	THE CLASS TRIP	#6	THE TWINS TAKE PARIS
#2	HOLIDAY MISCHIEF	#7	JESSICA'S ANIMAL INSTINCTS
#3	THE BIG CAMP SECRET	#8	JESSICA'S FIRST KISS
#4	THE UNICORNS GO HAWAIIAN	#9	THE TWINS GO TO COLLEGE
#5	LILA'S SECRET VALENTINE	#10	THE YEAR WITHOUT CHRISTMAS

Sweet Valley Twins Super Chiller Editions

#1	THE CHRISTMAS GHOST	#6	THE CURSE OF THE GOLDEN HEART
#2	THE GHOST IN THE GRAVEYARD	#7	THE HAUNTED BURIAL GROUND
#3	THE CARNIVAL GHOST	#8	THE SECRET OF THE MAGIC PEN
#4	THE GHOST IN THE BELL TOWER	#9	EVIL ELIZABETH
#5	THE CURSE OF THE RUBY NECKLACE		

Sweet Valley Twins Magna Editions

THE MAGIC CHRISTMAS	A CHRISTMAS WITHOUT ELIZABETH
BIG FOR CHRISTMAS	#100 IF I DIE BEFORE I WAKE